D0202232

Gypsy and the Moonstone Stallion

THE STALLION REARED . . .

as Wendy and her friends looked on, stunned by his breathtaking beauty. His pale coat was the color of glowing moonstone—just like that of the legendary Moonstone Stallion, the ghostly horse that was supposed to guard the burial place of the mighty Indian warrior who had ridden him a hundred years before.

Then the stallion vanished. Wendy and her friends searched the island, but they could find no trace of him. Only Gypsy, Wendy's beloved filly, seemed to know where the stallion was—but Gypsy couldn't tell Wendy what she knew.

Wendy had to find the stallion before it was too late. Soon Wild Horse Island, held sacred by Wendy's Indian friends, would be developed into a luxury resort, and the magnificent stallion would be destroyed—unless Wendy could find him first. Gypsy held the key. If only she could somehow tell Wendy where the stallion was hidden. . . .

Gypsy and the Moonstone Stallion

By SHARON WAGNER

Illustrated by Marilyn Hamann

Cover by Jean Helmer

GOLDEN PRESS
Western Publishing Company, Inc.
Racine, Wisconsin

© 1980 by Western Publishing Company, Inc.
All rights reserved. Produced in U.S.A.

GOLDEN® and GOLDEN PRESS® are trademarks of
Western Publishing Company, Inc.

No part of this book may be reproduced or
copied in any form without written permission
from the publisher.

0-307-21517-2

Contents

1   Indian Fair   11

2   Rodeo   27

3   A Call from the Past   42

4   Wild Horse Island   53

5   Gretchen   65

6   The Phantom Stallion   79

7   Bleak News   93

8   A Futile Search 104

9   Conspiracy 118

10   A Desperate Plan 130

11   Relic 145

12   Death Threat 158

13   The Stallion's Secret 172

14   Killer Stallion 189

15   Escape! 201

1 · Indian Fair

WENDY MCLYON stood at the corral, her arm over Gypsy's neck, as they watched the car drive away. "We'll miss them, won't we, girl?" she said to the chestnut Morgan filly. Gypsy whickered softly and rubbed her velvety nose along Wendy's arm.

"We all will," her uncle Art Roush said from inside the corral, where he was putting a halter on a two-year-old Appaloosa. "But it's nice that Joel and Fred will finally be back with their parents."

Wendy nodded, then laughed as her uncle handed Gypsy the lead rope and let the filly take the young horse to the gate. "I just didn't expect them to leave so soon," she admitted,

11

remembering the night less than a month ago when Joel had nearly died in a flood in Gulligan's Gulch. If it hadn't been for Gypsy and Nimblefoot's trust in her. . . . She shook her head. "At least the whole family is together now, so I don't think the boys will mind moving to California."

"And things can get back to normal here," her uncle said, haltering a second Appaloosa and bringing both horses out of the corral.

Wendy giggled, thinking that her uncle's idea of "normal" would have driven most people crazy. The Cross R was a guest ranch in the summer months, and now, the day before the Fourth of July, all three cabins were full. There were so many things that had to be done—rides to plan, cookouts, and trips to the national park for sightseeing, besides the necessity of fixing meals for everyone and keeping the cabins cleaned.

Still, for two hours every morning, Wendy spent her time helping her uncle train the young Appaloosa horses. That was the best part of her day, for she knew that what she was learning while training them, she would soon be using

12

with her own filly, Gypsy.

"You go see Nimblefoot, Gypsy," she ordered the filly, who ran loose in the home pasture most of the time. "I have to work now."

The filly looked at her for a moment with her mismatched blue and brown eyes; then she trotted over to where the black and white pinto gelding was standing with his head over the top rail of the big corral. The two horses touched noses, making friendly noises, and then stood watching as the two-year-olds walked, trotted, and cantered at the ends of the long lead ropes, or *longes*.

As she worked, Wendy continued to glance over at Gypsy, finding it hard to believe that the sleek, contented filly was the same creature she had found shortly after her arrival in Montana the previous April. They had both come a long way, she realized. Gypsy loved and trusted people again, and as for Wendy . . . well, she still wasn't perfectly comfortable riding, but at least she no longer remembered so clearly the horror of the accident in Phoenix that had killed her mount and made her vow never to ride again. She reached down to rub the leg she had injured

13

when her horse collided with the pickup.

"Hey, wake up there," Uncle Art called. Wendy snapped back to the present, realizing that the colt she was working was trotting instead of walking as she had commanded.

"Thinking about tomorrow?" Uncle Art asked as they stopped the horses and then led them over to the corral fence for the last part of their lessons.

"I guess so," Wendy said as she began picking up each of the colt's feet in turn, correcting him firmly when he tried to dance away from her. It was important for the horses to accept handling without trouble, and this was the only way to teach them.

"You don't have to ride in the barrel race if you don't want to," her uncle said. "You've proved that Nimblefoot has almost recovered. You have plenty of time for him to finish regaining his confidence."

"Maybe I'm the one that needs the confidence," Wendy suggested. "Besides, I want the people who saw him get so upset at the gymkhana to see that he's all well now."

Her uncle shook his head. "They won't

14

believe it," he said. "Sometimes I don't, myself. You have a real way with horses, Wendy."

"I just love them," Wendy said, blushing a bit at the praise. They released the last two horses in the corral, and Wendy turned her attention back to Gypsy, calling the filly to her.

"We may have to hire you out as a horse trainer next summer," her uncle said. Something in his tone made her look up at him.

"Why?" Wendy asked, petting Gypsy absently.

"From what I hear in town, we just might be getting some pretty fancy competition in the resort business," Uncle Art said.

"What do you mean?"

"Wild Horse Island has been sold to a Colorado corporation, and the talk is that it's going to be made into a resort."

"A dude ranch?" Wendy frowned, trying to remember the island. There were several islands on this side of the lake and more on the other side. She hadn't had a chance to explore any of them, except the one that they sometimes took guests to.

"It's not big enough for that," Uncle Art said, "but they can always rent horses at the stable in town, or they can even keep some there for their guests."

"Will it really make a difference to us?" Wendy asked, feeling cold inside. There had been so much change in her life. Her father's job had kept them moving through most of her twelve years. His acceptance of an overseas post shortly after her mother's death was the reason she had come to stay with Uncle Art and Aunt Laura. Now to think that this new life might be threatened, too. . . .

Her uncle grinned. "I don't think so," he said. "I guess I'm just sentimental. I hate to see that particular island torn up. It's sort of special, you know."

"How do you mean?" Wendy asked. Before her uncle could answer, she heard the loud clanging of the old-fashioned dinner bell that her aunt used to summon the guests, hired hands, and family members to meals during the summer.

"I'll tell you all about it later," Uncle Art promised. Wendy quickly put Gypsy in the corral with Nimblefoot and the other riding horses and ran toward the main house, aware that she'd have to wash and change so she could help Aunt Laura serve the noon meal.

There was no time to talk later, however, for right after lunch she and Uncle Art went into Littleville with the guests to see the Indian Fair. It was a splendid show, with colorful Indian dancers performing to the throbbing beat of their small drums.

There were eagle dancers, clad in feathered costumes, who made swooping and soaring motions, then ended their dance imitating the quivering and fluttering death of the sacred birds. Wendy felt sorry for the buffalo dancers sweating under the heavy buffalo hides as they moved through the streets.

Once the dancing was over, Uncle Art drove out to the vacant area near the Saddle Club grounds, where a number of the Indians had set up stands near their teepees. They displayed their crafts—intricate beadwork and fringed leather jackets, as well as baskets and beautiful woven blankets.

Wendy had as much fun as the guests, and it was hard to leave town early with Cliff, one of the two hired men who helped with the guests

17

and the ranch chores on the Cross R. But Wendy felt she should go back to the ranch to help her aunt with supper preparations. She was, she reminded herself firmly, a member of the family, not a guest. Aunt Laura's look of relief when she came in was her reward.

"You're back early," she said as she moved about the cheery yellow and green kitchen. "Don't tell me the guests got bored with the Indian Fair."

"I thought you could use some help," Wendy said. "I came back with Cliff in the pickup. He's going to feed the stock tonight so Uncle Art can stay with the guests."

Her aunt caught her in a quick hug. "Bless you, you must be a mind reader," she said, pushing back her hair. "This has been one of those days. I still haven't taken the lunch dishes out of the dishwasher or started to set up for dinner and. . . ."

Wendy smiled. "Leave it to me," she said, with only one longing glance out the window toward the green shadows of the forest that wandered so near to the ranch house.

"Now you know why we take things easy in

the winter," Aunt Laura teased. "It takes us nine months to rest up from summer."

"At least you don't have to cook much for the guests tomorrow," Wendy reminded her. "The Websters said they're going into town in the morning, and I think the Campbells may go with them, so that will just leave one guest family at lunch. Then everyone will stay in town for the barbecue after the rodeo, won't they?"

"They'd better," Aunt Laura said with a smile. "Tomorrow is my Independence Day, too, so there won't be anything to eat here."

They worked well together, Wendy emptying the dishwasher, setting the plank tables in the dining room, and then fixing the salad while her aunt took care of the main course. They were almost ready when the first of the cars drove past the window.

"You're more help than any three girls I've had before," Aunt Laura said, with a grateful smile.

The phone rang just as they finished dinner. Wendy hurried to answer it, since her aunt and uncle were both busy with the guests. It was

19

Wendy's friend Carol Carter. "Hi, Wendy," Carol said. "You busy?"

"We just finished dinner," Wendy said. "What's up?" She had grown very close to the slender brunet from the next ranch since the terrible day when Carol had helped her save Gypsy and a Morgan mare and foal from a late spring blizzard.

"My folks just decided to go into town for a while, and I wondered if you'd like to come along. We always go out to the Indian camp and visit. It's kind of neat at night, more like it was in the past, I guess."

"Sounds great," Wendy said, pushing back her dark blond hair. "Let me ask."

In a moment their plans were made. Wendy hurried to clear the tables and scrape and stack the dishes before going in to change. As soon as she was ready, she went out on the front porch to wait. Carol and her parents arrived almost at once.

Mr. Carter parked the car in town, and the four made their way through the crowded streets. As they neared the small gathering of teepees, Wendy couldn't believe her eyes. It was

20

like suddenly landing in the past. A large camp-fire burned in the center of the circle of teepees, and the Indians were dancing around it to the rhythm of a solemn chant.

"Do they do this every year?" Wendy asked as she and Carol drew closer.

Carol shook her head. "They have the usual dances during the day, like they did today, but this is special. Just listen to them."

Listening closely, Wendy noticed that the chant had a haunting, mournful quality to it. Also, the dancers' faces appeared solemn, almost grim.

"What's going on?" Wendy asked.

"I'm going to ask Little Elk," Carol said. "He'll know."

"Little Elk? An Indian?" Wendy was impressed.

Carol nodded. "He and his family live on the other side of the mountains, but they come here every year for the fair and rodeo. I always see him then, and they all stayed at our house one year when the fair was practically rained out. That's his father, Elk Tooth, leading the dancers." She pointed to a tall, spare man. He was clad in weathered buckskins and wearing a

21

magnificent feathered headdress that swung majestically as he shuffled in the dust and prairie grass.

Carol threaded her way through the crowd, and Wendy followed, glimpsing more of the dancers as they slowly circled the encampment. Most of the women wore buckskin dresses, beautiful creations with leather fringe and the wonderful beadwork that the Blackfeet were famous for.

"Hey, Little Elk, over here," Carol called, her voice rising above the steady throbbing of the drums and the somber chant.

A tall boy looked up, seemed to search the crowd for a moment, then grinned, his teeth very white against the red brown of his skin. He waved, then beckoned.

Carol moved through the crowd and slipped under the rope that kept people out of the encampment. Wendy hesitated at the rope, but Carol signaled her to come, so she slipped under it, too. The two girls moved into the shadow of the first teepee.

Little Elk came around from the other side, and in a moment Carol was introducing her

two friends. Wendy smiled shyly. "Come on inside," he said, leading them around to the second teepee and lifting the blanket that covered the opening.

Wendy followed Carol inside, then relaxed a little as she looked around. The outside might be authentic, but the inside made her feel at home. There were folding chairs and several lanterns. A camp stove sat off to one side, and there were folded cots stacked opposite it.

"What's going on, Little Elk?" Carol asked as they sat down on the floor, which was covered with a canvas tarp.

"It's a mourning dance for our ancestors who died on Wild Horse Island," Little Elk said. "Haven't you heard? Their spiritual resting place is going to be destroyed."

"I had heard that it was sold," Carol said, "but I didn't know— What do you mean, it's going to be destroyed?"

Little Elk shrugged. "I don't know the details, but my father is pretty upset. One of the things we always do when we come here for the fair is go out to the island at sunrise and say some prayers for the braves who died around here.

24

Next year the whole island will be completely changed."

They sat in silence for a moment, then Wendy said, "My uncle told me that he'd heard a corporation from Colorado was going to build a resort on the island."

"Then we have to go out tomorrow," Little Elk said, frowning. "This may be our last chance to pray for them in the traditional way."

"I'm sorry, Little Elk," Carol said. "I wish there was something we could do."

Wendy nodded, too shy to speak again. Suddenly the blanket flap of the teepee was lifted, and a woman peered inside. She smiled at the two girls, then turned to Little Elk. "Your father wishes you to join the dance, Little Elk," she said.

"I guess I'll see you tomorrow at the rodeo," Little Elk said, getting up at once.

"Good luck in the morning," Carol said as they followed the boy out of the teepee.

They made their way back into the crowd and watched the dancing with the others, but this time Wendy felt very differently about it.

No longer did it seem entertaining, for she now understood the sadness of the ritual. She was glad when Carol's mother suggested that it was time they went home.

2 · Rodeo

WHAT WERE YOU talking to Little Elk about tonight?" Peg Carter asked when they were back in the car.

Carol explained quickly, and Wendy asked, "What is the story about Wild Horse Island? Uncle Art was going to tell me this morning, but we never had time."

"Little Elk would be the one to ask," Peg Carter said. "I've heard a dozen different stories. It seems that a few Indian braves refused to be put on a reservation. They defied the cavalry and fled into the mountains. The soldiers weren't going to let them escape, though— there'd been too much trouble with the Indians—so they chased them unmercifully." She sighed and paused for a moment.

"The chief of the tribe was riding a magnificent stallion," Carol went on, "a pale horse the color of the moon. The horse was known as the Moonstone Stallion.

"The group made their final stand against the soldiers somewhere along the beach between our place and yours, and they were defeated. The men were willing to die, but the stallion plunged into the lake and swam out of sight with his rider clinging to his back. The stories say that the chief was wounded and died on the island, but the horse is supposed to still be on Wild Horse Island, guarding the final resting place of the chief who rode him."

"Then they really are just going out there to pray for the one man," Wendy said.

"Depends on the story," Mr. Carter said. "I've heard some people claim that the island is a real Indian burial ground and that the Moonstone Chief was just the last one to die there."

"Have you ever seen the horse?" Wendy asked.

Carol shook her head. "Some of the kids claim they have, but I haven't. We've been out

28

to the island a couple of times and have never seen a horse, even though there are signs that one has been there."

"Where is the island?" Wendy asked. "I mean, which one is it?"

"You can see it from the point," Carol said. "In fact, if you want to meet me there at sunrise tomorrow, we can probably see if Elk Tooth and the rest go out for their ritual."

"I guess I could," Wendy said. "We aren't going to be doing much tomorrow except getting ready for the rodeo. I'll ask Aunt Laura when I get home, and then give you a call."

"Are you still riding Nimblefoot in the barrel race?" Carol asked.

Wendy nodded. "Are you going to ride Quito?"

"Sure. I don't expect him to win, but it's good experience for him." Carol laughed. "I just hope he remembers he's not a bucking horse."

"Don't you both forget that you're out there to work," Peg Carter said with a smile. "I'm counting on you to make some money for the Saddle Club at the Pronto Pups stand."

"We'll sell so many hot dogs no one will even

want to go to the barbecue," Carol promised with a giggle.

Wendy just leaned back against the seat, sleepy and content. She'd been so lucky to make a friend like Carol, so that she could be a part of everything here. She was half-asleep when they reached the Cross R, but she gave Carol a call before she went to bed and promised to meet her at dawn.

It was cold and gray when the alarm shrilled in Wendy's ear, and for a moment she just stared at the dim world in confusion. Then she remembered Wild Horse Island and, sighing, left her comfortable bed and Little Bit's friendly purring.

She paused in the kitchen for a thick slice of homemade bread spread with butter and Aunt Laura's peach jam. Munching it, she headed for the corral, where Nimblefoot and Gypsy both whinnied greetings.

The ride to the lakeshore was pleasant, though the half-light was rather eerie and Wendy shivered in spite of her jacket. Everything was wet with dew. Gypsy bounded along beside Nimblefoot like a happy puppy, racing off to investigate things, then trotting back to touch the gelding's nose with her own.

When Wendy reached the lakeshore, she paused. The sky was turning pink and gold in the east, but the mist on the lake made the island invisible. Cliffs rose at the end of the beach, and Wendy had to guide Nimblefoot into the lake, skirting the cliffs till she reached the narrow spit of sand that formed the point. There she dismounted, petting both horses as she waited for Carol to appear.

Suddenly both horses lifted their heads, their ears at attention. Wendy looked up, expecting to see Carol coming around the cliffs on her side of the point, but then she realized that the horses were looking out toward the lake.

Strange sounds came from the mist, wailing and chanting and the pulsebeat of a drum. Wendy swallowed hard, shivering from more than the cold. At that moment, the first rays of the sun rose above the distant mountains, and the mist began to thin.

Carol came splashing up onto the sandy spit. "Sounds as if they're already out there," she said, sliding off Quito's brown and white back.

31

"Sorry I didn't get here sooner."

A breeze whispered around them, lifting the fading mist. Wendy could now see the dark bulk of the thickly forested island across the rippling blue of the lake. She could see no sign of the Indians, but she could hear their chanting rise and fall. After a few moments, a thin column of smoke spiraled up from the island.

"Did they really fight here?" Wendy asked, trying to see it in her imagination.

"Probably on our beach," Carol said. "I've found a couple of arrowheads there. Besides, the story I heard said that the horse disappeared from view, and you can't see the island from our beach."

"It's sad to think that they'll destroy all that, isn't it?" Wendy asked, staring at the island. "I mean, it seems so right the way it is."

Carol shrugged. "Maybe the Moonstone Stallion will stop them," she suggested.

"I hope—" Wendy began, then stopped as the roar of a boat motor cut through the stillness of the dawn. Both she and Carol turned to see a boat heading for the island. "I wonder who that is," Wendy said.

·"Probably the construction boss from town," Carol said. "It looks like his boat. The public docks are just beyond that ridge of trees to the left."

"Do you think he'll stop Elk Tooth and his people?" Wendy asked.

Carol shrugged. In a moment the boat had disappeared, and then the motor stopped. A few minutes later, the chanting ceased abruptly. Before very long, several canoes appeared from the far end of the island. As they paddled, the Indians in the canoes began to chant again. Hot tears of anger and sadness filled Wendy's eyes.

"I guess we'd better go home," Carol said, her tone telling Wendy that she felt the same sympathy for the Indians. "See you later."

Wendy nodded, the lump in her throat too big to speak around. She whistled for Gypsy and mounted Nimblefoot, waving to Carol as she headed the gelding back around the cliffs.

Why couldn't the construction boss have left the Indians alone? she asked the misty morning. What harm did they do by praying in the dawn for men who'd been dead probably close to a hundred years?

33

No one at the breakfast table had any answers for her, though everyone seemed to think it was wrong to send the Indians away. Uncle Art sighed. "It doesn't sound as if the new owner is going to be very neighborly," he said.

"It isn't the owner," Aunt Laura said. "A Mr. Underwood is in charge. At least that's what Mrs. Gleeson at the hotel told me."

"Well, the owner better come up here and start acting more like a resident," Uncle Art said. "The corporation should send a representative. Those Indians have been making that prayer ritual on the island for as long as I can remember, so they should have some rights."

When they reached the Saddle Club grounds a little after noon, Wendy was amazed. Though the rodeo didn't begin till one, it was already a madhouse. Uncle Art had a hard time finding a place to park the pickup with the horse trailer so they could unload his Appaloosa stallion, Happy Warrior, and Wendy's Nimblefoot.

"I'll take Nimblefoot down and tie him near the contestants' entrance," Uncle Art said. "I can keep an eye on him while I'm in the arena."

"I wish I could watch you and Happy," said

Wendy. "I've never really noticed what a pick-up man does."

"I just help the riders off the bucking stock," Uncle Art said. "Actually, Happy does most of the work."

"You'll have time to take a couple of breaks during the afternoon," Aunt Laura said. "I always schedule plenty of people to work. Once the big rush is over, we take turns wandering up in the stands."

"I didn't mean that I didn't want to work in the booth," Wendy hastened to assure her aunt.

Aunt Laura laughed. "I know what you meant," she said, "but come on, I've got to get the batter ready and heat up the deep fryers."

The Pronto Pups booth was located under the grandstand, and even with an electric fan, it was soon very hot, but everyone giggled and laughed as they fastened the hot dogs on sticks, dipped them in batter, and quick-fried them in the hot oil. Wendy sampled her first efforts and found them delicious.

The first rush of customers lasted for well over an hour. Then Aunt Laura fried up a few batches of Pronto Pups and sent Wendy and

Carol into the stands with them. It took Wendy quite a while to sell hers, because she spent more time watching the action in the arena than she did looking for hungry customers.

She was very glad that her hands were free when the winners of the calf roping were announced. She applauded Kirk Donahue, the red-haired nephew of the town's veterinarian, when he rode out to accept third prize. Kirk had been her first friend in Littleville, and she knew how hard he'd worked training his bay, Apache, for the event.

"I hate to go back," Carol said, joining her at the top of the grandstand just as the bareback riding was announced.

"The first rider will be Little Elk Porter on Chain Lightning, coming out of chute one," the announcer said. Both girls paused on their way down.

"I didn't know he was riding this year," Carol said. "He's only fourteen."

The chute opened, and Wendy gasped as the small buckskin burst into the arena, bucking wildly. It twisted, sunfishing to show a pale golden belly, then reared and leaped forward to

buck again. Little Elk was almost lost in the heavy, dark mane for a moment, then he was clearly visible, one hand waving clear, his feet moving in the proper rhythm to score points.

The buzzer ended the ride after what seemed an eternity. Wendy let her breath out slowly as Uncle Art maneuvered Happy Warrior alongside the buckskin so that Little Elk could swing over the stallion's haunches and drop to the ground on the far side, away from the bucking horse's deadly hooves. The announced score brought shouts and whistles from the crowd.

"He's going to be hard to beat," Carol said with a smile. "That's the best score I've heard in years, and that buckskin has a bad reputation 'cause he twists instead of bucking straight."

"I'd hate to try to ride him," Wendy agreed as they headed reluctantly back to the booth. It seemed hotter than ever inside, now that they'd been in the stands, and Wendy insisted that Aunt Laura and some of the other women take a break.

By the time the girls' barrel racing was called, they were nearly out of hot dogs. Wendy wasn't sorry to see that Aunt Laura and Mrs. Hammer

38

were beginning to pack things up. This was the last event of the day, so there were few customers.

Uncle Art was standing at the contestants' gate, petting the two pintos while Happy rested. The stallion's black coat was streaked with dust and dried sweat, and his white-spotted haunches were still shiny from the wiping they'd received from the cowboys sliding across them.

"Looks like the hot dogs weren't the only things getting fried in that booth," Uncle Art observed with a grin. "Hot work?"

Wendy nodded. "Next time I think I'll volunteer for your job—that looks a lot cooler."

He handed her Nimblefoot's reins. "Your friend here has missed you," he said. "And probably Gypsy, too. This is the first time they've been separated since you started riding him, you know."

"I hated to leave her home," Wendy agreed, mounting the gelding and moving him around to limber up. Carol joined her on Quito, and in a few minutes the horses were dancing and moving into line with the other contestants.

Carol rode fourth, and as expected, Quito

was too excited, bumping the first barrel and knocking it over to disqualify himself. Nimble-foot bounced with excitement as they moved forward in the line of riders.

Wendy felt a stirring of fear in the pit of her stomach, remembering how he'd behaved at the gymkhana; then she relaxed, sure that his fears were behind him now. When her name was called, she rode him into the arena, paused, then leaned forward, heading for the first barrel at a full gallop.

Nimblefoot made the first turn so tight that Wendy's toes set the barrel to rocking, but it didn't go over. They made it around the second turn safely, and the third was easier. She leaned forward, urging him to top speed as they passed the timers, then pulled him into a fine, sliding, cowpony stop. Applause rang in her ears. When she heard her time, she gulped with shock. It was the best so far, and there were only three riders left!

The next horse was faster, but poorly trained, losing precious seconds on the turns; the one following knocked over a barrel, and the final horse was too slow. "Show-off," Carol teased as

Wendy's name was announced as winner.

As Wendy rode in to accept the ribbon and trophy, she glowed with pride, not for herself, but for Nimblefoot. He was no longer the frightened, undependable horse he had become after the serious accident he'd had the previous summer.

"Boy, we'll really have to celebrate tonight," Carol said as they rode away from the arena together. "I'm going to feel kind of out of place, though. You and Little Elk both won in your events, and Kirk was third in the roping." She sighed, then giggled. "I guess I'm just a failure."

"Fast as Quito is, we won't stand a chance, once you get him trained," Wendy acknowledged. "By next year we'll all be eating your dust."

Carol patted the young pinto's shoulder. "He's learning," she said. "It just takes time."

"See you at the barbecue," Wendy said, stopping beside her uncle's horse trailer.

"You bet," Carol agreed, riding on to where her folks were waiting for her.

3 · A Call from the Past

THE DOWNTOWN AREA was seething with people by the time Wendy arrived, feeling a little strange in the full-skirted blue print peasant dress that Aunt Laura had helped her make for the occasion. Wendy seldom wore dresses, still conscious of the scars on her knee from the pickup accident, but tonight everyone seemed to be dressed up in country style.

Music blared, and the scents drifting from the city park, where two whole steers had been roasting in pits throughout the day, were enough to revive the dead, Wendy decided, her stomach rumbling in response. Carol, wearing a similar dress of yellow and orange print, was standing near the end of one of the food lines.

42

The two girls quickly picked up plates and moved along to be served potato salad, molasses-sweet baked beans, garlic bread, and huge slabs of barbecued beef.

"Now where?" Wendy asked, holding her heaping plate with both hands.

"Over under the trees," Carol said. "Kirk's going to meet us there. He said he has a big surprise."

They found a spot well shaded from the setting sun and settled themselves, starting in on their food at once so it wouldn't get cold. Before they'd taken a dozen bites, a familiar voice said, "I told you we'd find them already stuffing themselves."

Wendy looked up and was surprised to see not only Kirk but Little Elk as well, both of them carrying heavily laden plates. She congratulated them on their rodeo performances as they sat down.

Carol waited till the boys were settled, then asked, "Is Little Elk your surprise?"

Kirk grinned, his blue eyes dancing. "Sort of. He's going to be staying with Uncle Hal as an assistant. Little Elk is planning to become a

43

veterinarian when he gets out of college."

Little Elk nodded. "That's why I had to win today," he said. "Dr. James will let me live and work with him, but I'll need money for school in the fall. The purse from the rodeo is as much as I could earn in weeks working for my father at home."

"You can learn a lot in two months," Kirk added.

"I'd want to stay here, anyway," Little Elk said firmly, his face changing. "Someone has to."

"What do you mean?" Kirk asked.

Little Elk looked around, then lowered his voice. "Our tribe is very upset about what's happening to the island." He shook his head. "I promised my father that I'd return to the island and try to find a relic that was left by our ancestor. He feels that if we could take something that belonged to the Moonstone Chief into the mountains and give it proper burial, his spirit would rest—no matter what that construction boss does to the island."

"Was it the construction boss who ordered you off the island this morning?" Wendy asked.

Little Elk nodded, his eyes boring into her. "Where were you?" he asked.

"We were watching from the point," Carol explained. "We saw the man go out to the island, and then your people left."

"He said it was private property, that we were trespassing." Little Elk's tone was bitter, but then he grinned. "Maybe the Moonstone Stallion will make him pay for what he's doing to the island."

"Have you ever seen him?" Wendy asked. "The stallion, I mean."

Little Elk shook his head. "Only his hoofprints and the signs of his grazing."

"Then you really think there is a horse on that island?" Kirk asked. "I always figured it was just a legend."

"I never heard of a legend that left tracks," Little Elk said.

"Why don't we go out and look for ourselves?" Carol suggested.

"To the island?" Wendy asked. "But what about the—the contractor, I think Aunt Laura called him? He wouldn't want us on the island, either."

45

"We could go out Saturday," Kirk said. "I don't think they work on the weekend. It wouldn't really be trespassing; we won't bother anything."

"If we go from our beach, no one will see us," Carol said. "We can use the canoes."

"You have canoes?" Wendy asked, surprised.

"Two of them," Carol said. "We used to paddle out there for picnics and stuff, but since I've been working with Quito, I just haven't had time this year. What do you think? Can you go Saturday, Wendy? Little Elk?"

Wendy thought for a moment, then nodded. "I'm free in the morning and for most of the afternoon, too. Uncle Art and Aunt Laura are taking the guests to Glacier Park, so I don't have to be back till time to start dinner."

Little Elk only shrugged. "It depends on Dr. James," he said quietly.

"If we tell him it's a picnic, he'll let us both go," Kirk said. "He gives me two days off a week; they just don't get planned. If there aren't any emergencies, Saturday should be fine."

"Well, let's finish our food and go see how the street dance is," Kirk said, turning his attention back to his plate. "Do you know how to square dance, Wendy?"

Wendy shook her head, feeling shy again.

"Well, you'll have to learn," Kirk said. "Okay?"

The street dance was fun, and after her first awkwardness, Wendy soon managed to learn enough of the steps to take her place with the others in a square. She was very sorry when Aunt Laura came for her at ten-thirty, saying that they had to be getting home. It was hard not to envy the guests when she looked back to see them still dancing and laughing. They wouldn't have to rise early to feed the horses or fix breakfast. She stifled a sigh, then grinned, remembering that they would be leaving in a few days or a few weeks, while she'd still be here.

When they got home, they found a note the hired man had left on the kitchen table. Aunt Laura picked it up with a yawn, then handed it to Wendy. "Looks as if you're the popular one," she said.

Wendy stared at the note for a moment, then swallowed hard.

There was a long distance call for Wendy at 7:30, it read in Cliff's scrawl. *Call Operator 4 in Phoenix before ten, or the party will call again tomorrow.*

"It's too late to call tonight," Wendy said after a moment.

"Do you think it might be your friend Gretchen?" Aunt Laura asked.

Wendy nodded, not sure how she felt about it. "I invited her to come up here for a visit this summer," she said. "I mean, you said it would be all right and. . . ."

"Of course it is," Aunt Laura said. "Your friends are always welcome here. You know that."

"I wonder if her parents decided to let her come," Wendy mused. When she had issued the invitation, she had meant it, of course, but. . . . Well, now she remembered only too well how miserable she'd been when she left Phoenix. She remembered, too, how Gretchen Simpson, once her best friend, had turned against her after Gretchen's horse had been killed through Wendy's carelessness.

"How would you feel about having her here?"

48

Aunt Laura asked, following Wendy down the hall to the room she had decorated for her.

Wendy sighed. "I'm not sure now," she admitted. "When she wrote and asked me to forgive her for the way she acted after the accident, I really meant it when I said that I did, but now. . . . Everything's going so well and. . . . I just don't know."

Her aunt nodded. "I think it will work out," she said. "You have a whole new life here to show her—it won't be like it was in Phoenix. You've both grown up since then."

"I'm just afraid that seeing her will bring it all back," Wendy admitted.

"It's always bad when a friend hurts you," Aunt Laura said, "but you have Gypsy and Nimblefoot and all your friends here, so I think you're ready to face whatever comes. Just don't worry about it tonight. We have a long ride arranged for tomorrow, you know, all the way to High Meadow."

Wendy nodded. "I guess it's a good thing I'm going to be busy."

"Just remember, I'll be here to help," her aunt said, kissing her good night.

"Thank you," Wendy said as her aunt left the room.

Though she tried to follow her aunt's advice, Wendy found sleep a long time coming. Next day, the ride seemed to take forever. She was proud of the way Nimblefoot handled the rocky terrain, and she welcomed the diversion Gypsy offered as the playful filly accompanied them to the beautiful meadow high above the lake, but she was glad when it was time to start home.

All day she had tried to think what she'd say to Gretchen, but when the phone finally rang at seven-thirty, she went to answer it still undecided.

"Wendy, is that you?" Gretchen's voice sounded small and far away.

"Hi, Gretchen," Wendy said. "I'm sorry I missed your call yesterday, but we didn't get home till almost eleven and—"

"That's okay. I knew you were going to be busy. I mean, you told me in your letter about the rodeo and everything. How was it? Did your horse do all right in the barrel racing?"

"He won first," Wendy said, some of the strangeness slipping away. "He's a terrific

50

horse, you'll just love him and. . . ." She let it trail off, realizing what she'd said. "You did call to tell me that you're coming, didn't you?" she asked after a moment, knowing at last that she did want to see Gretchen again.

"Do you still want me to?" Gretchen sounded timid, shy in a way that was totally new to Wendy.

"Of course," she said. "When can you come?"

"Would Sunday be all right?" Gretchen still sounded unsure of herself.

"That would be great," Wendy said. "What time does your plane get here?"

The arrangements were quickly made, and all too soon, Wendy replaced the receiver. She turned to find her aunt standing behind her, her eyes full of questions.

"She's coming on Sunday, about four-thirty," Wendy said. "She can stay two weeks. Is that all right?"

"How do you feel about it?" Aunt Laura asked.

"Sort of scared, but glad, too."

"Then it's just fine. We'll have a welcome-to-the-ranch party Sunday night. We can ride to

51

the beach and have a campfire there. Do you think she'd like that?"

Wendy nodded, then gave her aunt a quick hug before returning to the living room and her knitting. She was just starting a sweater, having finally finished a pair of slippers for Uncle Art and a pair for herself. She was grateful to Aunt Laura for having taught her to knit, since she had a feeling she'd be chewing her nails if her hands weren't busy.

4 · Wild Horse Island

FRIDAY DRAGGED BY as Wendy worked with the horses, helping Uncle Art catch up on the training that they'd neglected for the past two days. As they worked the two-year-olds, she tried to picture Gretchen here, wondering if she'd like to help, too.

She was glad when Carol called in the afternoon to say that she'd just talked to Kirk and they were all meeting at her house about ten Saturday morning. Going to Wild Horse Island would make the waiting much easier, Wendy felt.

The sun was bright and warm Saturday morning as Wendy, Nimblefoot, and Gypsy neared the Carter ranch. Kirk and Little Elk were already busy carrying a red canoe out of the Carters' garage, and Wendy could see a second canoe resting on the sand, waiting for them.

"Sorry I'm late," she said.

"There's no rush," Carol assured her, bringing out a big basket. "I just finished packing our lunch."

"I should have come sooner to help you," Wendy said, feeling guilty.

"Oh, come on," Carol said. "Kirk and Little Elk were here early enough to make sandwiches. They brought a watermelon, too, so we'll have lots of food."

"You sure it's safe to go over?" Wendy asked, looking toward the lake.

"Nobody's come out today," Carol said. "I've been watching. I can't see the town docks or the island, but you can't get from one to the other without going past here."

"We saw Mr. Underwood—he's the contractor—when we came through town," Kirk said. "Come on, put your horses in the corral, and let's go. I can't wait to see if we can find the Moonstone Stallion."

54

Wendy unsaddled Nimblefoot and put him and Gypsy in the corral with the other horses, then started toward the beach. Gypsy began to whinny immediately, and when Wendy looked back, she saw that the filly was at the corral gate working on the latch with her slim muzzle.

"She's going to turn the horses loose," Wendy warned as the filly released the latch and pushed the gate open with her chest.

"I thought she didn't do that anymore." Carol stopped, too.

"She hasn't for a long time," Wendy said, turning back with a sigh. "I don't know what's wrong with her today. She's been kind of silly ever since I left her home on the Fourth. I think she's jealous because Nimblefoot got to go with us."

"Why don't you just leave her out of the corral?" Carol suggested, following her back. "She won't wander away from Nimblefoot, will she?"

"She never has," Wendy said, closing the corral gate before the other horses followed the filly out. She gave the filly a smack on the haunch. "You behave yourself, Gypsy," she ordered.

55

Gypsy bounded away, then turned back as though expecting Wendy to chase her. Wendy just shook her head as she and Carol joined the boys on the beach.

"She's like a dog," Little Elk observed as he and Carol dragged the first canoe out into the lake.

"Sometimes too much so," Wendy agreed as she helped Kirk with the second canoe, nearly upsetting it as she tried to climb in. Gypsy had followed them to the shore and now stood there with her front feet in the water, looking very much as though she wanted to go with them.

"You stay with Nimblefoot, Gypsy," Carol called. "You're too big to ride in a canoe."

Laughing, Wendy accepted a paddle from Kirk and tried to copy the way Carol was paddling in the front of the red canoe. It took her several minutes to master the stroke. Meanwhile, she was conscious of Gypsy's whinnies from the beach. When she looked back again, she was startled to see that the filly was now chest-deep in the water.

"I think she's going to follow us," she said, forgetting to paddle. "What'll I do?"

56

"Not much you can do," Kirk replied, "unless you want to go back and put her in the corral again. We could tie it shut, I suppose."

"She'll probably give up pretty fast," Little Elk said. "Most horses don't really like to swim."

They paddled in silence for several minutes, and then Wendy looked back again. At first she didn't see Gypsy at all, but then she saw the sorrel head rising above the blue of the lake. Gypsy was following them, and she showed no sign at all of turning back!

"What if she comes out to the island?" Wendy gasped, looking back at Kirk.

He shrugged. "Maybe she'll be able to find the stallion for us," he suggested.

It seemed to take forever to reach the patchy sand and rock that formed the nearest shore of the island, and Wendy watched Gypsy's progress rather fearfully. The filly had dropped back a little, but she swam steadily. Shortly after they'd pulled the two canoes up out of the water, she came wading ashore, looking very pleased with herself as she shook water on the four of them.

58

"Show-off," Wendy said, hugging the horse's wet neck. "What do you think you are, a sea horse?"

Gypsy blew softly through her nostrils, nudged Wendy, then lifted her head and looked at the tree-covered island, her ears sharply forward as though she had heard something. She whinnied loudly.

"Let's look for him," Kirk said.

Gypsy trotted away from them, disappearing into the trees almost at once. Wendy led the way as they hurried after her, everything else forgotten.

The island was beautiful. The trees gave way to small meadows carpeted with grass and wild flowers, then closed in again to shade them as they followed the filly. The ground rose sharply toward the middle of the island, and Wendy caught the sound of falling water as they crossed a final meadow. They neared a grove of trees that grew at the base of what looked like a rocky hill. Here the filly stopped, looked around, then whinnied plaintively.

"You can see that a horse has been here," said Little Elk. "See the tracks? And the grass has

59

been eaten down here, too. It's much shorter than it was in the smaller clearings we came through."

Wendy looked around and saw that he was right. "So where is he?" she asked.

"I don't know," Carol said, "but I wish we'd brought the basket with us. This is a perfect place for our picnic."

Wendy followed her gaze and saw that there was a small pool among the trees on the far side of the meadow. Then she saw the source of the sound she had heard. A waterfall spilled down from the cliffs above, feeding the pond and the little stream that ran from it to the lake. "It's beautiful," she murmured.

"This is the sacred place," Little Elk said, his voice suddenly changed. "It must have been somewhere around here that the Moonstone Chief died. This is where we come to offer our prayers."

Wendy nodded, seeing the small dark circle in the grass where the fire had been built. She could almost hear the chanting, haunting and alien as it had been at dawn on Wednesday. She shivered, feeling like an intruder in this place.

60

"Are we going to look for the stallion?" Kirk asked, his strained tone telling Wendy that he, too, was feeling the eeriness of the location.

"You go ahead," Little Elk said. "I'd like to stay here for a while, if you don't mind."

Kirk, Carol, and Wendy exchanged glances, then nodded. "We'll get the lunch," Kirk said. "You just wait here."

The rest of the island was similar to what they'd already seen, except that as they neared the end of the island that faced the town docks, they began to see the marks of the future. Stakes had been driven into the pine-needle-coated ground, and there were ropes joining them, marking out what, Wendy assumed, would be the hotel that was to be built here.

There were further signs that a horse had been on the island, but no matter where they walked, they saw no living creature larger than a squirrel or chipmunk. They circled back, following the shore till they reached the canoes once again. Only then did Wendy look around, realizing that she hadn't seen Gypsy since they left the clearing where Little Elk had remained.

"Do you think we should go back now?"

Wendy asked. "I mean, I feel sort of funny about leaving Little Elk."

"He's probably getting hungry by now," Kirk said, picking up the watermelon from where they'd left it in the cold lake water. "I know I am."

"It makes me feel bad to think what they're going to do to this island," Carol said, her dark eyes meeting Wendy's blue ones. "It's so pretty and peaceful. It just seems wrong."

"Especially if it *is* an Indian burial ground," Kirk agreed. "They don't have any right to destroy something like that."

"And what about the stallion?" Wendy asked. "If they build a hotel here, what will happen to him?"

No one had any answers. After a moment, Carol and Wendy picked up the basket between them, and Kirk followed with the watermelon. To Wendy's surprise, they found both Little Elk and Gypsy still at the pool.

"Did she stay here with you all the time?" she asked Little Elk as Gypsy came to sniff at the picnic basket.

Little Elk nodded. "She started to follow you,

62

then came back and just grazed here while I looked around."

"Find anything?" Kirk asked.

Little Elk shook his head. "I don't even know what I'm looking for," he admitted with a grin. "My father just said that the Moonstone Chief would have brought with him to the island whatever he treasured most, and since this is to be destroyed, it's only right that his relics should be saved."

"We could help you look," Carol suggested.

"After lunch," Little Elk agreed, the strain easing for all of them. "Right now I'm practically starving."

As they ate, Wendy told them about Gretchen's coming visit. Kirk was full of suggestions for things they could do during the two weeks Gretchen would be staying, and Wendy grew more excited herself as they talked. It would be fun, she decided.

Though they searched the island again after they ate, they found nothing, except for one arrowhead that Kirk picked up on the beach. Still, as they paddled back across the open stretch of water to the Carter beach, Wendy felt better.

Only Gypsy seemed disturbed, standing on the shore of the island for a long time before she finally plunged in to follow them.

"Guess she's learned her lesson," Kirk observed with a laugh. "She won't be so eager to swim after us, now that she knows she's going to have to swim back."

"Don't count on it," Wendy replied. "You have to remember that she thinks she's one of the group."

"She is," Carol called from the other canoe. "She's our mascot, remember?"

They all laughed, but as she stared at the distant shore, Wendy found herself wondering about Gretchen. Would she be one of the group, too? The next day she would find out. The next day Gretchen would arrive!

5 · Gretchen

By FOUR-THIRTY Sunday afternoon, Wendy was too nervous to sit still in the small airport where she had arrived what seemed like so long before. Remembering how frightened she'd been then, she wondered how Gretchen was feeling. She found herself rubbing her right knee often and thinking too much about the past. It was almost a relief when she heard the sound of the plane as it came over, banked, and dropped down on the landing strip.

Aunt Laura stayed back, forcing her to greet Gretchen alone. Wendy went out, searching the passengers for a familiar face. Gretchen came down the plane steps slowly, her hazel eyes going over a crowd while she apprehensively pushed at her reddish brown hair. The last of Wendy's anger and worry about the meeting drained away as she recognized her friend's fear; her smile was full of forgiveness as she waved and called Gretchen's name.

"You're taller," Gretchen said as Wendy hugged her.

"You cut your hair," Wendy answered, aware that neither one of them was saying what she was thinking.

"I've been swimming a lot," Gretchen said, pushing again at the untidy riot of waves and curls. She looked around and took a deep breath. "It's so cool here," she murmured. "It was a hundred and ten when we left Phoenix."

"You'll freeze to death," Wendy teased. "Come on and meet Aunt Laura. Uncle Art couldn't come; he's getting things ready for the steak fry."

"Steak fry?" Gretchen still looked a little uneasy.

"We're having a welcome-to-the-ranch ride and dinner by the lake for you," Wendy said. "Everybody is looking forward to it. We'll have a big fire and sing and tell ghost stories and. . . .

66

Well, it should be a lot of fun."

"You really like it here, don't you?" Gretchen asked, her face sober.

Wendy looked around, then nodded. "It's home," she said simply.

The first strain eased as they drove back to the ranch. There were so many things to point out to Gretchen—the Saddle Club grounds, rather empty now without the Indian teepees; the school; the small shopping area of Littleville; the ranches they passed on the way to the Cross R. Wendy found herself talking more than she had in years, but she couldn't seem to stop. She wanted Gretchen to love it here as much as she did.

At the ranch she introduced Gretchen to her uncle, to George and Cliff, the two ranch hands, and to the guests who were present. Then she took her down to the corral to see Gypsy and the other horses.

"This really makes me feel at home," Gretchen said, petting the friendly noses that were poked over the corral fence. "It must be neat to live right here with the horses."

"It's a lot more work," Wendy replied.

"Training and feeding and everything." She described what she'd been doing with the two-year-olds.

Gretchen scratched behind Gypsy's ears. "You'll be experienced at training by the time Gypsy is old enough to ride, won't you?" Her tone was envious.

"None of them are like Gypsy, anyway," Wendy said with a sigh. "Uncle Art says she doesn't know she's a horse. She thinks she's a person."

"She's beautiful. It's too bad about her eyes, though. I mean, you could show her in Morgan shows if she didn't have that blue eye." Gretchen stepped away from the fence. "Did I tell you that I've asked Daddy for a half-Arabian? I'm going to show it in all the shows around Phoenix."

Just then, Aunt Laura called them in to change for the ride. There was no time to think about anything but getting things ready. There were horses to be saddled for the guests, and Wendy had to help Gretchen choose a mount for the ride.

Once they reached the lake, Wendy found

herself busy helping her aunt and uncle with the cooking and with serving the guests, so she had little time to spend with Gretchen. She was glad then that her aunt had invited Carol to join them and to meet Gretchen.

Still, as she watched her two dearest friends, Wendy soon sensed that something was wrong. She had no chance to find out what it was, however, till she and Gretchen lay in her soft bed with Little Bit and Abigail purring between them.

"So what do you think?" she asked. "Are you glad you came?"

"It's fantastic," Gretchen said, but her voice betrayed an edge of doubt. "But are you always so busy?"

"I'm sorry about tonight," Wendy said. "Things should be a little easier next week. The Websters are leaving in the morning, and I don't think the cabin is rented yet."

"If you'll tell me what to do, I'll be glad to help," Gretchen said. "I mean, your aunt and uncle are really nice."

"How did you and Carol get along?" Wendy asked. "Did she tell you about Quito?"

"I don't think she likes me," Gretchen said. "She hardly said a word."

"She's kind of shy," Wendy said, frowning into the darkness, "except when it comes to horses."

Gretchen said nothing, and Wendy wondered what had happened between the two girls. The silence lengthened, and finally Wendy took a deep breath and asked the question she'd been dreading to ask. "How . . . how are things in Phoenix? I mean . . . with my . . . friends."

Gretchen turned over, petting Little Bit. "They feel just like I do, Wendy. We were rotten to you, and we'll never forgive ourselves for the way we acted after your accident. We shouldn't have blamed you for what happened to Buck."

"I took him out of the riding area," Wendy admitted painfully. "I'd been warned."

"We all did it," Gretchen reminded her. "It was an accident, pure and simple. It could have happened to any one of us."

Wendy blinked back tears, touched by the way Gretchen was willing to share her guilt. "How are all your horses?" she asked.

70

Gretchen sighed. "They're fine, but I think I might sell all but one if I get the half-Arab. I don't have too much time to ride now, and if I'm going to show a horse, that takes a lot of time."

"I suppose it does," Wendy said, closing her eyes, suddenly very tired. Everything seemed the same and yet so different with Gretchen. *It'll take a while before we're as close as we used to be*, she decided before slipping off to sleep.

Monday dawned sunny and warm. By the time the guests had been served breakfast and the two cabins were made up, Wendy was feeling much better. Since there was no guest ride scheduled, she was pleased that she and Gretchen could spend the entire afternoon just riding around the ranch; there was so much she wanted her to see.

She and Uncle Art were just showing Gretchen how to train the two-year-olds, when a car came bouncing along the road toward them. Uncle Art looked up, then frowned a little before handing Wendy the lead rope of his colt. "That's Sheriff Ramsey," he observed, going to meet him. "I wonder what he wants."

Wendy tied the colt to the corral fence, then was startled to see the sheriff and her uncle coming her way. Her uncle beckoned to her, so Wendy patted Gypsy and walked over to them. "The sheriff wants to talk to you, Wendy," her uncle said.

Wendy looked up at the bulky man. "Is something wrong?" she asked.

"I think you know the answer to that," Sheriff Ramsey said. "You were out on Wild Horse Island Saturday, weren't you?"

Wendy winced, gulped, and then nodded. "We had a picnic out there," she admitted.

"And you took a horse with you?" The sheriff's face was solemn.

"Well, not exactly," Wendy said. "I mean, we didn't intend for Gypsy to go, but she swam across, following the canoes." She paused, then sensing that something was wrong, asked, "Why?"

"Who all was with you?" Sheriff Ramsey asked, not answering her question.

"Carol Carter, Kirk Donahue, and Little Elk Porter," Wendy answered reluctantly. "Why, Sheriff? What's wrong? We just had a picnic by

the pool there. We didn't hurt anything."

"A picnic by the pool? Are you saying that you weren't on the south end of the island at all?" The sheriff's questions were relentless and without explanation.

"Well, not exactly," Wendy replied. "I mean, we did explore the whole island. We were looking for the Moonstone Stallion."

"On an island you knew was closed to the public?"

This time Wendy felt the blood rising in her cheeks. "We didn't hurt anything," she stated. "It was just a picnic, that's all."

"That's not what Mr. Underwood says," Sheriff Ramsey snapped, his expression grim. "He came to my office this morning and took me out to the island. I saw what you kids did, Wendy, and I don't blame Underwood for being upset. He spent most of last week setting out those stakes."

"What are you talking about?" Wendy asked, shocked out of her momentary feelings of guilt. "We saw the stakes, but we didn't touch them."

The sheriff's frown deepened. "If you didn't tear them up, who did?" he asked. "There were horse tracks all around. It looked like maybe your filly got caught in the ropes and started kicking. Everything was torn up."

Wendy relaxed for the first time. "Gypsy wasn't at the south end of the island, Sheriff," she said. "You can ask Little Elk. He stayed by the pool and Gypsy stayed with him."

"Could I see your filly?" the sheriff asked.

"Of course." Wendy whistled, and Gypsy came trotting over. "She didn't do it, Sheriff."

Sheriff Ramsey inspected the filly thoroughly, running his hands down her slender legs, then picking up her hooves to check them. Finally, he sighed. "She does have mighty small hooves," he said. "A lot smaller than the tracks by the stakes. But where the devil would another horse come from?"

"We found a lot of horse tracks on the island," Wendy said. "That's why we were looking for the Moonstone Stallion."

"That's just an old legend," the sheriff replied. "Besides, if there was a horse on that island, don't you think Underwood would have seen it? He's been spending every day on the island for a week now."

75

"But you do believe Wendy, don't you?" her uncle asked, speaking for the first time.

The sheriff sighed. "The filly's hooves are too small, and she has no rope burns. Besides, I just don't see Wendy as a vandal."

"None of us did anything like that, Sheriff," Wendy repeated. "We just explored the island and ate a picnic lunch, and then we came back home."

"What about Little Elk?" the sheriff asked. "You said he stayed by the pool."

Wendy returned the sheriff's gaze boldly, her usual shyness banished by her anger. "Little Elk probably stayed by the pool to finish the prayers that his family had been saying the morning Mr. Underwood ordered them off the island. He didn't even see the dumb stakes."

The sheriff winced. "I didn't like that, either," he admitted, "but Mr. Underwood was perfectly within his rights. They were trespassing on private property."

"It was their island first," Wendy reminded him.

"Not really. The fact that one renegade Indian chief died there doesn't make it an Indian burial ground. That's the only thing we know to be true. The other stories. . . . Well, the Blackfeet buried their dead in trees and—"

"Trees?" Wendy gasped.

The sheriff nodded. "They put them on platforms in the trees—mostly to keep them away from wild animals, I suppose. Anyway, any trace of such burials would be long gone, so. . . ."

"But the Moonstone Stallion isn't," Wendy reminded him. "You saw the tracks."

"I saw horse tracks," the sheriff agreed, "but more than that. . . ." He shrugged. "All I'm saying is, you keep that filly off the island and stay off it yourself. I don't want any more trouble. Is that clear?"

Wendy nodded, swallowing more protests, more words about the mysterious stallion.

The sheriff nodded. "All right, I'll talk to the others. The Indian boy is working for Dr. James, isn't he?"

Wendy nodded again, wishing that she didn't have to. She felt sorry for Little Elk and was glad that the sheriff had come here first so she could tell him that Little Elk hadn't even seen the stakes. She watched the sheriff till he got in his car, then turned back to face her uncle.

"Want to tell me about it?" he asked quietly.

"It's just like I told the sheriff," Wendy said, petting Gypsy. "We didn't touch the stakes, Uncle Art, honest."

"I know that," he said, "but you'd better be careful. I don't want any trouble with Mr. Underwood. I know you're in sympathy with Little Elk and his people, but there's nothing you can do." He grinned at her. "Now let's get these horses exercised so you can show Gretchen the rest of the ranch. We'll be bringing in the horse herd tomorrow, Gretchen, so you can look them over when you're out there today and see if you find any you think you'd like to try."

"Thank you, Mr. Roush," Gretchen said, but her eyes were on Wendy, and Wendy could see the curiosity glowing in them. Wendy winked at her, then went to get the filly she'd left tied to the corral fence; explanations would have to wait till after the training session was done.

6 · The Phantom Stallion

THE AFTERNOON PASSED almost too quickly for
Wendy. Riding with Gretchen and telling her
all about the mysterious Moonstone Stallion
and the visit to Wild Horse Island seemed to
bring back their old closeness. They even rode
out to the point to look at the island.

"I wish I could go out there," Gretchen said.
"I'd love to see it."

"If the sheriff hadn't come—" Wendy began,
then stopped as Gypsy began to whinny and
waded out into the lake, her full attention on
the distant island.

Almost at once, an answering neigh came
across the water, and a pale horse suddenly
emerged from the trees. Wendy gasped as the

horse reared, whinnied once more, then spun around and disappeared back into the undergrowth.

Gypsy plunged forward into the water and began swimming toward the island. For a moment, Wendy was too shocked to act, but then she regained her senses and whistled. The filly slowed, her delicate ears turning first toward the island, then back to Wendy. "Come on back, Gypsy," Wendy called. "Come on, girl."

The filly seemed to hesitate for a moment, then slowly turned back. She waded ashore and shook off the water before sending one last whinny toward the island. This time there was no answer.

"What was that?" Gretchen asked.

"The Moonstone Stallion," Wendy breathed, shaking her head. "He exists, Gretchen. He's really out there!"

"So what do we do now?" Gretchen asked, kicking Soot, the gelding she was riding, into a canter to keep up with Wendy and Nimblefoot.

"We've got to go home and tell Uncle Art," Wendy said. "The contractor has to be told about the horse. They'll have to get him off the island before they start building there. He could get hurt."

"Well, at least that clears Gypsy's name," Gretchen said. "I mean, in case the contractor doesn't believe the sheriff."

"I can hardly wait to tell Carol and Kirk and Little Elk," Wendy went on, her mind bounding ahead. "They've never seen him."

"The Moonstone Stallion," Gretchen murmured. "He really looked pretty, even from so far away."

Wendy nodded, her thoughts busy planning exactly how she'd tell Uncle Art. Meanwhile, she was keeping an eye on Gypsy. The filly had been willing to swim out to the island without her, Wendy realized, and that worried her.

When they got home, Uncle Art listened to their story, then said, "You're sure, Wendy? You didn't just see something and imagine . . . ?"

Wendy shook her head. "We heard him whinny—he was answering Gypsy—and then he came out on the beach for a moment. He looks as if he's about the same size as Happy, only not so heavy, and he's the strangest color, sort of a misty cream or gray."

"The color of a moonstone," Gretchen said. "I've seen bracelets and stuff that are made with what they call moonstones, and he was that color; but he was a real horse. We both saw him."

"Then I'd better call Mr. Underwood," Uncle Art said. "I just wonder where the devil that horse has been hiding. You don't suppose he swims back and forth, do you?"

Wendy gnawed at her lip. "Have you ever heard of a horse like that around here?" she asked after a moment.

Uncle Art frowned, then shook his head. "There are a couple of white horses, but one is a mare as old as our Ladybug, and the other is Tom Raither's gelding and he's never running loose. I can't think of any others. Why don't you call Carol and check with her? Maybe she knows of some that I don't."

When Wendy called and asked, Carol's answer was quick and to the point. "There aren't that many white horses around. Nobody in the Saddle Club has one, except Mr. Raither. Wendy, that has to be the Moonstone Stallion. He must have been on the island all the time."

Wendy sighed. "He must be awfully wild to hide from us."

"What do we do now?" Carol asked. "The sheriff must have told you to stay off the island; he sure made it clear to me."

"Uncle Art is going to call Mr. Underwood," Wendy said. "They'll have to search the island and get the horse off before they go ahead with their construction."

"I wonder what they'll do with him," Carol murmured.

Wendy giggled. "If Gypsy gets close to him, she'll probably bring him home," she suggested. "She was ready to swim out to see him."

"It's funny she didn't find him Saturday," Carol said.

"He must have been hiding from her, too," Wendy replied, but her own doubts rose with the words. If she hadn't seen the stallion so clearly . . . hadn't heard him. . . .

"How about some help in here?" Aunt Laura called from the dining room as soon as Wendy hung up the phone. "We've got to get the tables set before a lot of hungry people pour in."

Wendy worked quickly, her mind still on the

call her uncle was making. When he came into the dining room, she turned to him, her work forgotten. "What did he say?" she asked.

"Well, he wasn't convinced, but he did agree to search the island before they start work in the morning."

"He didn't believe you?" Wendy frowned. "Why not?"

Uncle Art sighed. "I think he—well, he thought you made it up because he saw you out on the island with Gypsy."

"I wouldn't do that," Wendy protested.

"I know that, but he doesn't. All he knows is he saw you kids paddling out to the island with a horse when he was out fishing Saturday morning, then Monday morning he found hoofprints in the middle of a torn-up construction site. I'm afraid he's not feeling very friendly toward you."

"What will he do with the horse if he finds him?" Wendy asked, not liking what she was hearing.

Her uncle shrugged. "I offered to help him get the horse off the island, but I don't know if he'll call or not."

84

"What about the owner, Mr. Roush?" Gretchen asked from the other side of the room. "Could he do something?"

Uncle Art shook his head. "The owner is a big corporation. I'm afraid they wouldn't be much interested in the fate of one very elusive horse."

"Maybe we should go out and—" Wendy began.

"No," Uncle Art said firmly. "That's the one thing I don't want you to do. Mr. Underwood's parting words were for me to keep you and your horse off *his* island, as he called it. I think we've done all we can for the moment. In the meantime, we have to get Cabin Three ready after dinner."

"Somebody coming?" Wendy asked.

"Mrs. Gleeson called from the hotel. She's overbooked, and she wants us to take a couple that are flying in from the east. It seems that somebody left the water running in one of her rooms during the rodeo, and the overflow soaked through and weakened the ceiling so badly in the room below that she's going to have to have some work done before she can rent either room."

"How long will they be here?" Wendy asked —not really caring, but wanting to take her mind off the horse on the island and what might happen to him tomorrow.

"Maybe just overnight," Aunt Laura said from the doorway. "They may not be too thrilled at being on a dude ranch instead of in town."

"We'll just have to make them feel welcome," Uncle Art said. "I'd sure like to keep the cabins full, and we don't have another reservation for two weeks."

"When do they get here?" Wendy asked.

"I'm going to meet the plane about noon tomorrow," Aunt Laura said, "so I'm afraid you'll have to handle lunch. Think you can manage?"

Wendy nodded. "Gretchen can help me," she assured her aunt, with a glance at her friend.

"I'd go," Uncle Art said, "but Laura is so much better at meeting people."

"Coward," Aunt Laura teased.

"Well, we do have to bring in the horses in the morning, and then I'll have to take the others out, and I promised Mrs. Vincent that she could try a new horse, and. . . ." He let it trail off, laughing with the rest of them.

Wendy smiled, but her thoughts were still on the horse she and Gretchen had seen. She suddenly wished that she hadn't told anyone but Carol and Kirk and Little Elk. In spite of what the sheriff had said, she had a feeling that if they went out to the island. . . .

The evening sped by as they prepared the cabin and planned for tomorrow. Wendy and Gretchen would help Cliff and George bring the horses in, giving Gretchen a chance to try some of the other horses before she decided if she wanted to keep the black gelding, Soot, as her permanent mount during her stay.

In spite of everything she had to do, Wendy found her thoughts wandering toward the island as they rode into the lake pasture the next morning. She longed to make the trip to the point to look for the stallion, but she knew there was no time. With Aunt Laura gone, she would have to go to work in the kitchen as soon as they got back. She wouldn't even have time to help Gretchen pick a horse.

They were just starting the herd toward the ranch when Carol came galloping along the shore on Quito. "I was just riding over to see if you'd heard whether Mr. Underwood found the horse," she said.

Wendy shook her head. "We haven't heard so far, but from what Uncle Art said, I don't think we will."

"What do you mean?"

"He didn't believe me," Wendy said with a sigh.

"You mean he doesn't think there is a horse?" Carol was frowning.

"Oh, he said he'd search, but I don't know. We searched the island and didn't see him," Wendy reminded her, admitting to her fears.

Gretchen reined Soot in beside the two pintos. "Did you see him on your way over?" she asked Carol.

Carol shook her head. "Maybe he isn't there."

"We saw him," Gretchen snapped. "We weren't dreaming."

Carol glared at her. "I know you did," she admitted coldly. "I was just thinking about all the stories. I mean, maybe he really is the Moonstone Stallion."

"We said that," Gretchen reminded her. "So

88

why should that mean he isn't there?"

"The Moonstone Stallion is supposed to appear magically just to protect the dead chief," Carol explained. "Maybe that was what he was doing."

Wendy sighed, not liking the coldness between her two friends, but not sure how to change it. "I wish that was it," she said. "I wouldn't worry about him if he was just a legend."

"You think he's real?" Carol asked.

"Gypsy does," Wendy replied, "and she hasn't even heard the stories."

"So what do we do?" Carol asked.

Wendy shrugged her shoulders. "I don't know," she admitted.

They rode in tense silence for a moment, then Wendy had an idea for dealing with her immediate problem. She smiled at Carol. "Do you think maybe you could help Gretchen pick a horse to ride?" she asked. "I've got to get lunch ready as soon as I get back. Besides, you know the horses better than anybody but Uncle Art. He's going to be busy looking for a horse gentle enough for our guest Mrs. Vincent, but not one so quiet it falls asleep while she's *oh*ing and *ah*ing over her eternal wild flowers."

Carol giggled. "That's going to take some work. I've seen your Mrs. Vincent ride."

"I think I'll probably just stick with Soot," Gretchen said, ignoring the peace offer. "He's nice to ride."

"He is a good horse," Carol agreed, "but there are a couple more in the herd that should be more fun for you. He's so well trained, he's not much of a challenge."

Gretchen stiffened. "I thought we were just riding to have fun," she snapped.

Wendy opened her mouth, but before she could say anything, Uncle Art was yelling at them to get back to watching the horses. She had to ride off to bring back several of the horses who had followed Gypsy away from the herd.

Carol immediately dropped back to keep the slower horses moving. Gretchen and Carol were still on opposite sides of the herd when Wendy rode ahead to open the gate of the corral. A chorus of whinnies came from the young horses in the barn. In a moment, Gypsy disappeared

91

into the barn, while the horse herd filed into the corral.

Wendy followed Gypsy, unsaddled Nimble-foot, and put him in a vacant stall before she went up to the house to fix the lunch. As she looked back at the corral longingly, she could see Gretchen sitting on the corral fence while Carol rode Quito back the way she'd come. She sighed, wondering if the two girls would ever make friends. At the moment it seemed very doubtful.

7 · Bleak News

LUNCH KEPT WENDY too busy to worry about anything. Though there were only eight guests plus the family and hands, it was her first time fully in charge, and even Gretchen's help wasn't enough. By the time everything was on the tables, she was shaking with the strain and far too tired to enjoy her own food.

"I don't know how Aunt Laura does it," she confided to Gretchen as she sank down beside her at the family table. "I mean, this is just lunch, and I almost forgot the bread, and I still don't have the puddings ready for dessert, and besides. . . ."

"Take it easy, honey," Uncle Art said. "Nobody expects everything to be perfect.

You've done a great job. Laura will be proud of you."

"Did you pick a new horse to ride, Gretchen?" Wendy asked, after a few minutes.

"I decided to keep Soot," Gretchen said, her eyes on her plate.

"Didn't Carol have any suggestions?" Wendy frowned at the stubborn tone in Gretchen's voice.

"She had to leave," Gretchen said.

"You can still try a couple this afternoon, if you like," Uncle Art suggested. "We don't have to turn them out right away."

"It really doesn't matter," Gretchen said. "Soot is fine for the riding we do. I'm not selecting a show horse or anything."

Uncle Art shrugged. "It's up to you, Gretchen," he said. "We just want you to have a good time."

Wendy sighed and reached for the butter just as the telephone rang. She started to rise, but Uncle Art waved her back into her chair. "I'll get it," he said. "Maybe it's Laura saying that our guests are getting back on the plane."

Wendy took another bite, conscious that the

guests at the other tables were already well along with their meal and that she'd have to go back to the kitchen in a few minutes. Her spirits began to rise as she realized the lunch was nearly over, then dropped again when she saw her uncle's expression as he returned to the table.

"Something wrong?" she asked.

He sighed. "That was your friend Underwood."

"The stallion?" Wendy's heart skipped a beat.

"He says that there is no horse on the island and that we're never to bother him again. He's lost half a day of work, and he's very angry." Uncle Art dropped down into his chair. "Are you two really sure you saw the stallion?"

Wendy looked at Gretchen, then nodded. "He was there," she assured him. "And he may still be there."

"Underwood said they went over the whole island."

"He hid from us," Wendy reminded him.

"Well, there's nothing more to be done," her uncle said. "He must have left the island. Maybe he swims to shore and hides someplace in

that public land. You know how rough it is—
no one rides through there much."

Wendy nodded, but deep inside she was sure
that he was wrong, and that thought frightened
her. She finished her food in silence. She was
just ready to get the dessert when they heard a
car.

Uncle Art went to the window, then called,
"Better set up another table, Wendy. Laura's
here with our new guests."

Wendy hurried to the kitchen and checked to
be sure that there was plenty of food left for the
newcomers. She carried two more place settings
into the dining room, setting the fourth table
quickly and efficiently. She had everything
ready by the time Uncle Art and Aunt Laura
came in with the Montgomerys.

They were a handsome couple, apparently
about the age of her aunt and uncle, but dressed
in clothes more suited to a city than to a ranch.
The woman looked around the room, and Wendy could see the disdain in her face even before
her voice revealed it. "This is your dining
room?" she asked.

"My wife is the best cook in Littleville, Mrs.

96

Montgomery," Uncle Art said. "If you'd just like to sit down. . . ."

The woman looked as if she might refuse, but her husband smiled easily, though the warmth of it didn't reach his eyes. "Sit down, Pamela," he said. "You'll feel better after you've had something to eat and then maybe a little nap."

"I slept on the plane," Mrs. Montgomery said coldly. "What else is there to do around here?"

"Do you ride?" Uncle Art asked.

Mrs. Montgomery's nose twitched. "Horses?"

Wendy suppressed a giggle, but several of the guests' children laughed out loud, and Wendy could see the anger burning in the woman's face. Mr. Montgomery moved quickly to seat his wife, while Wendy followed her aunt into the kitchen, where they both laughed silently till their sides ached from the strain.

"It's going to be an interesting few days," Aunt Laura said when she caught her breath.

"They're going to stay that long?" Wendy asked, surprised. "I thought maybe they were just waiting for a plane back."

"Mrs. Montgomery would have gotten back on the one they came in," Aunt Laura said with a wry smile, "but her husband has some kind of business here, so she's going to have a 'new experience.' And so, I'm afraid, are we. I don't know what I'm going to do with her."

Wendy just shook her head, unable to offer a single suggestion. They finished lunch in a rather tense atmosphere, only too conscious of Mrs. Montgomery's murmured complaints about everything from the decor to the seasoning of the casserole that everyone else had loved. It was a relief to leave to her aunt and uncle the chore of helping the Montgomerys move in. Meanwhile, Wendy and Gretchen finished separating the selected horses from the herd and prepared to drive the rest back to the lake pasture.

As they worked with Cliff and George, under the curious eyes of the guests, Wendy had no chance to talk to Gretchen about the plan forming in her mind. However, once the horses were on their way back to the pasture, she reined Nimblefoot over beside the black gelding.

"Let's ride on over to Carol's after we leave the herd," she suggested.

Gretchen frowned. "Why?"

"Because we've got to do something about the

Moonstone Stallion," Wendy explained.

"What?" Gretchen asked. "I thought your uncle said he'd left the island."

"I don't think so," Wendy said. "If he was going to leave the island, he could have come to see Gypsy yesterday. He seemed to want to."

"So where was he when they were searching the island?" Gretchen didn't sound convinced.

Wendy sighed. "Probably hiding the same place he was when we were over there Saturday."

"Then why don't we just go over and look?" Gretchen suggested. "Why do we need Carol?"

"Because we can't swim that far," Wendy said, her temper flaring, "and Carol has the canoes. Besides, she and Kirk and Little Elk are just as interested in the stallion as we are, and it'll take all of us to find him." She paused, then asked, "Just what do you have against Carol, anyway?"

Gretchen shrugged. "She acts as if she's the only person in the world who knows anything about horses. Just because she's training that scrubby pinto. . . . When I get my half-Arab. . . ."

Wendy sighed. "Quito is half Quarter Horse,

99

and he's going to be a super gymkhana horse. Up here, that's more important than being a show horse. There just aren't that many horse shows in this area."

"Sure, take her side." Gretchen reined Soot away.

For a moment Wendy just glared after her, but then her thoughts went to the pale horse on the island. She held in her anger, kicking Nimblefoot after her. "Gretchen," she said, "I'm not taking sides. I'd like you and Carol to be friends, for my sake; but if you can't, please, could we try to work together—for the sake of the horse on the island?"

For a moment she could see the stubbornness in Gretchen's hazel eyes. Then it faded, and her grin replaced it. "I'm sorry," she said. "I guess maybe I could try again—if she isn't too stuck-up to speak to me."

"When I tell her what Mr. Underwood said, I'm sure she'll be more interested in the stallion than in fighting with you," Wendy assured her, hoping fervently that it was so. She remembered only too well the way Carol had ridden off this morning without saying good-bye.

GYPSY AND THE MOONSTONE STALLION

They settled the herd in the pasture, then rode on to the beach and started toward the point. Gypsy began to whinny at once, and there was an immediate answer, but not from the island. Quito's brown and white head came poking around the rocks, and in a moment they joined Carol on the point of sand.

"See anything?" Wendy asked immediately.

Carol shook her dark head. "I thought maybe they would be herding him this way, you know, to get him off the island; but I haven't seen anything, not even the construction crew."

"They aren't going to be herding him off," Wendy said with a sigh. "Mr. Underwood called at noon and said that they didn't find any horse. He doesn't want to hear any more about it."

"They didn't find him?" Carol frowned. "But. . . ."

"They probably didn't look very hard," Gretchen observed, sliding off Soot. "I mean, he's not exactly small, and that island doesn't look so big."

"What are we going to do?" Carol asked, ignoring Gretchen's words, her dark eyes meeting Wendy's and reflecting the same worry that

101

Wendy was feeling at that moment.

"I think we ought to go back out and try to find him again," Wendy said. "We could take a rope and bring him back with us. Then he'd be safe."

"What about the contractor?" Carol asked.

Wendy looked around. "If we left from our beach instead of yours, we'd be pretty hard to see from anywhere but the island."

Carol considered for a moment, then nodded. "When?"

"Tonight. After it starts to get dark." Wendy gnawed at her lip. "How about having a wiener roast on the beach? I'm sure my uncle and aunt would understand. We could invite Kirk and Little Elk, too. That way the three of you could come by canoe. Do you think your folks would mind?"

Carol grinned. "Heck, no. It sounds like fun. I mean, it would be fun if it weren't for the stallion."

Wendy nodded. "I'll go home and talk to Aunt Laura and Uncle Art; then I'll call you to let you know for sure. Could you call Kirk and Little Elk? I don't want my aunt or uncle to know about our going to the island, so I can't phone from home."

"Mom's in town, and I don't suppose Dad will be home till later, so I can call the boys," Carol agreed. "Call me as soon as you can."

They parted quickly, new purpose speeding them on their way. Still, as they rode back along the beach, Wendy cast a last glance at the island, wondering once more if the elusive Moonstone Stallion was really out there. Did he really exist, or was he just a phantom from the past?

8 · A Futile Search

WENDY FELT VERY GUILTY, because her aunt and uncle not only agreed to the wiener roast on the beach but also seemed happy that she was planning such an outing. If it hadn't been that the stallion's life might be in danger. . . .

Packing the hot dogs and buns, the containers of macaroni salad, the cookies, and the other goodies that emerged from the refrigerator and freezer, she wished mightily that she could confide in her aunt, but there was too much at stake. Once the stallion was safely off the island, she promised herself firmly, then she would confess everything. In the meantime. . . .

"How are the new guests?" she asked.

"Out, thank heavens," Aunt Laura said with

a smile. "As soon as the grand lady stopped complaining long enough to go to sleep, Mr. Montgomery asked to be taken to town so he could rent a car. When he got back, he informed me that they would be having their dinner this evening.

Wendy giggled. "I hope they eat at the hotel; then maybe they'll appreciate your cooking more."

"The decor should suit them," Aunt Laura agreed, "but I'm not sure about the rubber chicken, undercooked peas, and cold mashed potatoes Mrs. Gleeson specializes in."

"I've heard that the construction crew have taken their business to the High Top Coffee Shop," Uncle Art contributed from the doorway. "They were getting too weak to work."

"I wonder what kind of business Mr. Montgomery could have here," Wendy mused. "He sure doesn't look as if he belongs in Littleville."

Aunt Laura frowned. "Do you think it could have something to do with the hotel on Wild Horse Island?" she asked after a moment.

Wendy paused in her packing, her heartbeat quickening at the suggestion.

105

"Why do you say that?" Uncle Art asked, leaning on the door frame.

"I don't know. That's just the only new thing going on here. I mean, no one would take Mr. Montgomery for a cattle buyer."

They all three laughed easily. Then one of the guests came in to ask about tomorrow's ride, and Wendy turned her attention back to packing the saddlebags. "Don't forget the marshmallows," Aunt Laura called as she went to the stove to check the dinner.

"Got them," Wendy replied. "See you later."

"Have fun, and don't stay too late," Aunt Laura said. "We're going on an all-day ride tomorrow, you know."

"Don't worry about us," Wendy answered. "We'll just hang around the beach and sing, probably, or tell ghost stories."

"Or watch for the Moonstone Stallion?" Her uncle's tone touched her shoulders with a chill.

Wendy shrugged. "We did see him," she reminded him, "no matter what Mr. Underwood says."

"It's out of our hands now," Uncle Art said. "But the horse has lived out there for a long
106

time, so he'll probably just swim to shore and turn up in somebody's pasture sooner or later. Don't worry about him."

Smiling and waving, Wendy hurried out the back door, feeling too guilty to comment. Gretchen followed her with a sigh. "I feel awful fooling them," she confessed as they went to the corral for the horses.

Wendy nodded. "We'll tell them as soon as we get the horse off the island," she assured her friend. "We just can't tell them now—you heard Uncle Art. He'd never let us go out there tonight."

Carol, Kirk, and Little Elk were waiting on the beach when they rode down, and the fire was already burning brightly. Introductions and dinner preparations eased the first minutes, and by the time they were ready to devour the piles of food, Wendy was happy to see that the presence of the two boys had lessened the strain between Carol and Gretchen. She had a feeling that they all had to work together if they wanted to save the horse on the island.

Once the sun dropped below the mountains on the far side of the lake, Kirk swallowed one

107

last marshmallow, sighed, and got up. "I think it's dark enough now, don't you?" he asked.

Wendy nodded, her eyes on the distant shadowy island. "I just hope it isn't too dark to find the horse," she said. "I didn't even think about that."

"It always looks darker from here," Carol assured her. "We've got quite a bit of twilight left." She looked around. "Ready?"

"Let me get the rope from my saddle," Wendy said.

As they paddled across, Gretchen riding in the canoe with her and Kirk, Wendy surveyed the lake and the shore in every direction. She remembered only too well that they'd been seen by Mr. Underwood while he was fishing, and she was afraid that it might happen again, especially when Gypsy stood on the shore whinnying piteously as they rowed away.

"Call her," Kirk said. "Maybe she can help us find the horse."

Wendy started to whistle, but before she could make a sound, a loud neigh rang out from the island. They all looked up to see the pale horse as it broke out of the trees, galloped a few

108

strides on the beach, then stopped to whinny again. Gypsy answered at once, plunging into the lake to follow the two canoes as they headed for the island!

The stallion spun around and galloped back toward them. Then he reared and, after a final whinny, disappeared into the trees. The silence he left behind was broken only by the soft sounds of their hurried paddling and Gypsy's snorting and splashing after them.

"He's magnificent," Kirk said, his voice hushed. "No wonder you were so excited when you saw him."

"He looks even better this close," Wendy admitted, "but wilder."

"Well, this time we should be able to follow him," Little Elk said.

"Or Gypsy," Carol added. "He seems very interested in her."

"He's probably lonesome if he's been on the island for a long time," Wendy observed. "You know how much horses like to be together." She dug her paddle in deeper, her shoulder muscles aching with the strain.

In spite of their efforts, the filly reached the

shore just a few seconds after they pulled the canoes up onto the sand. Wendy tried to catch her, but Gypsy disappeared into the trees without even stopping to shake the water from her sorrel coat.

"What now?" Gretchen asked, looking at the others.

Wendy peered into the brush, but there was no sign of the filly. "We can't follow her," she said. "We'll just have to find them."

Kirk looked around. "If we spread out, we could be pretty sure that we wouldn't miss them. The island isn't that wide."

Little Elk nodded. "Wild as that stallion is, he's going to take off if we get close, so we'll hear him, even if we don't see him."

"You girls take the middle," Kirk said. "I'll take one side, Little Elk, and you take the other." He started off along the shore. "Give a yell if you see anything," he called over his shoulder.

Gretchen followed him about halfway along the shore, then turned into the trees. Carol did the same in the other direction, leaving Wendy to go down the middle of the island. She followed

111

as closely as possible the way Gypsy had gone. Wendy started forward slowly, suddenly feeling apprehensive of the darkness that lay beneath the trees. She was uncomfortably aware that this had been her idea and that she had to see it through.

For the first few minutes, she could hear both Carol and Gretchen as they pushed their way through the underbrush. Then, as the island grew wider, the sound faded and she was seemingly alone in the silent forest. Should she call Gypsy, she asked herself, or would that just frighten the stallion away?

The darkness eased ahead, and she broke out into the welcome light of a meadow, looking around at once for a sign of the horses; but there was nothing. Sighing, she plunged ahead, hurrying toward the next band of trees, knowing that eventually she would reach the pool and somehow sure that she would find the horses there.

There were no shouts to destroy the stillness as she neared the clearing by the pool. Wendy paused at the edge of the trees, conscious that she didn't want to frighten the stallion if he was here. Almost at once she heard a scratching sound from across the clearing. Something was moving over near the pool.

"Gypsy," Wendy called softly, straining to peer through the shadows. She was sure that she would have seen the pale horse if he had been there, but she felt that the dark-coated Gypsy could easily be hidden in the gloom. "Where are you, girl?"

The sounds stopped at once. Wendy waited for a moment, then slowly, carefully, crossed the open area, heading for the pool, convinced that the horses must be there somewhere.

It was very dark under the trees, and as she got closer, the steady noise of the waterfall blocked any other sounds she might have heard. Wendy hesitated at the edge of the trees that bordered the pool. Again she strained her eyes into the darkness, sensing something there, but unable to see what it was.

Suddenly a whinny broke the stillness, and Wendy heard the rattle of hooves on the rocks to her left. Before she could turn, something struck her in the middle of the back, propelling her violently toward the pool. She screamed as her right knee twisted painfully, then she splashed into the water, which broke her fall.

Gretchen and Carol arrived before she could clamber out of the pool. Their hands were welcome as she limped up the slippery bank. Almost at once, a soft muzzle rubbed on her shoulder. Wendy slipped an arm over the filly's neck, leaning part of her weight on Gypsy's withers.

"What happened?" Carol asked. "Did you fall in?"

Wendy closed her eyes for a moment, her mind suddenly filled with the memory of the eerie chanting she and Carol had heard at dawn on the Fourth. She shivered, not just from the aftereffects of the cold pool water. "Something pushed me in," she said at last.

"What's going on?" Kirk came pounding out of the trees to join them. A moment later Little Elk came panting from the other direction. He pulled off his sweater and handed it to her.

"What happened?" Little Elk asked. "How did you get so wet?"

Wendy took a deep breath, trying to make sense out of her own wild imaginings. "I'm not

114

sure," she admitted after a moment. "I thought I heard something over here, but when I got to the edge of the trees there, I couldn't see anything, so I stopped. I think I called Gypsy, but. . . ."

"Did she push you in?" Gretchen asked, her tone disbelieving.

Wendy shook her head emphatically. "Just before it happened, I heard her coming from over there." She pointed toward the hill and the waterfall. "Whatever hit me was behind me." Wendy looked toward the trees on the other side of the pool.

"Could it have been the stallion?" Little Elk asked.

Wendy considered for a moment, then shook her head again. "It wasn't a horse," she said. "I don't know what it was, but it wasn't a horse."

"So what do we do now?" Carol asked.

"We've got to get Wendy home before she catches cold," Gretchen said immediately.

"But the stallion—" Wendy protested.

For a moment there was silence, then Little Elk stepped forward. "How would it be if Kirk and I finish the search? You girls could paddle

115

back to the beach and build up the fire—give Wendy a chance to dry out."

Wendy nodded. "I sure can't go home this way," she agreed with a sigh. "But if you find the stallion. . . ."

"We'll handle it." Kirk was firm. "You three go on back to the beach."

"I could stay and help," Carol said, "if Wendy and Gretchen can go alone."

Kirk shrugged. "Can you handle the canoe, Wendy? Gretchen?"

"We'll manage," Gretchen said. "You just find the stallion."

"What about Gypsy?" Carol asked. "What's she doing here without the stallion?"

Wendy shrugged. "I wish I knew," she said. "Do you want me to leave her here?"

"Why don't you just let her make that choice?" Carol suggested. "If she follows you back, okay. If not, maybe she'll go looking for the stallion again."

"Good thinking," Wendy said, starting slowly back across the open area, leaning heavily on Gypsy as her knee throbbed with every step. "Just so she gets me to the shore."

116

At the shore, Gretchen helped Wendy into the canoe, then pushed it laboriously out into the lake before climbing in herself. There was an immediate splashing behind them, and as they paddled for shore, Gypsy swam alongside, obviously no longer interested in the mysterious pale stallion she had followed into the trees less than an hour before.

Is it because he's hidden again? Wendy asked herself. *And if he has, what will become of him tomorrow or the next day, when the construction crew finds his hiding place?* She shivered and paddled harder, longing for the warmth of the fire they had left burning in the sand.

9 · Conspiracy

WENDY'S CLOTHES were nearly dry by the time the second canoe came gliding back across the inky blue lake, but her spirits hadn't risen. No matter how many times she went over what had happened, it made no sense. She wasn't the slightest bit surprised when the three searchers reported no sign of the pale horse.

"So now what?" Kirk asked, sinking down on the sand. "What do we do next?"

Wendy shook her head. "I wish I knew. We can't keep coming back every night, but—"

"Where could he hide?" Little Elk asked, staring into the fire. "We looked everywhere. I'd swear that there wasn't a horse on that island, but we all saw him."

118

"How's your leg?" Carol asked.

Wendy shrugged. "I just twisted it. It'll be all right in a day or so."

"And you're sure that something pushed you?" Carol murmured.

Wendy nodded. "No matter how much I think about it, it doesn't change. Something—or somebody—pushed me into that pool."

Little Elk sighed. "Maybe we're worrying about nothing," he said softly. "Maybe the pool has its own protection."

"What are you saying?" Kirk asked, frowning.

Little Elk shrugged, looking rather embarrassed. "I never believed much in the legends and all that. I mean, they're old traditions and I honor them, but. . . ." He looked around rather hopefully.

"Are you saying that maybe the stallion isn't—well—a living horse?" Wendy asked, understanding his feelings.

Little Elk grinned. "Did you ever see a horse disappear that way before?" he asked.

"That wasn't any ghost on the shore," Wendy protested.

Little Elk sighed. "So where did he go? And

what pushed you into the pool?"

Wendy shook her head, then got painfully to her feet. "I don't know, but I think we'd better be getting home. I don't want Uncle Art coming out looking for us."

"I'll call you tomorrow," Carol promised. "Maybe we'll think of something."

"Make it late," Wendy said. "Tomorrow is an all-day ride."

"I don't think you'll be going," Kirk observed, moving to help her mount Nimblefoot, "not with that leg."

"Oh, a good night's rest—" Wendy began, then winced as she tried to put her foot in the stirrup. "They need me."

"I'll bet Gretchen could handle it," Carol said, in what was obviously a peacemaking gesture. She turned to the girl who was mounting Soot. "Couldn't you, Gretchen? I mean, you helped out with the riders at your father's stable, didn't you?"

Gretchen looked startled for a moment, then she, too, seemed to see the significance of Carol's words. A smile spread over her face. "I'd sure like to try," she admitted, "if your leg

120

is really bothering you, Wendy, and if you think it would be all right with your aunt and uncle. They've been really nice to me, so I'd like to help."

"You just may get your chance," Wendy conceded, shifting her weight to ease the angle of her leg. "I don't think I'd be much help on a ride."

"What are you going to tell them about your leg?" Gretchen asked as Wendy whistled for Gypsy and reined Nimblefoot around.

"That I stumbled and twisted it and fell in the water," Wendy replied.

"You don't think we should tell them about the stallion?" Gretchen asked.

Wendy closed her eyes. "What good would it do?" she asked. "We didn't find him."

Kirk's words proved prophetic. When Wendy got up the next morning, her leg was far too stiff to tolerate riding, and it grew little better as she limped about her chores. Everyone was very concerned, but she quickly eased their worries. After a great deal of their fussing, she watched as they all rode away, leaving her alone in the silent, empty house.

Bored, Wendy retired to the small room opposite her aunt and uncle's bedroom. She'd had little time for sewing since the beginning of summer, but as she looked at the material and patterns stacked in the crowded area, she couldn't work up any enthusiasm. Her thoughts returned to the horse on the island and to what had happened to her at the pool.

She'd heard something first, she was sure, but not the sounds a horse would make. She closed her eyes, concentrating her full mind on remembering. The sounds had been partially masked by the rushing of the waterfall, but. . . . *Digging!* she thought at last! That's what the sound had been. Someone had been *digging* near the pool!

The memory filled her with excitement, banishing her feeling that perhaps some Indian spirit had attacked her. Spirits wouldn't be digging, she was sure, and that meant that someone else had been on the island last night. Her sore knee forgotten, she hurried out of the sewing room and down the hall toward the kitchen, anxious to call Carol and see what she thought of the new information.

"I've never been any place like this." Mrs. Montgomery's outraged voice stopped Wendy in the hall. She paused to listen.

"Pamela, I told you to stay in New York," Mr. Montgomery said. "I warned you that this was purely business."

"You didn't tell me we'd be trapped in the wilderness," Mrs. Montgomery complained. "They've all gone off without a care. We could starve to death, and no one would notice."

"I have to make a call, then I'll drive you into town for lunch."

"Not at that abominable hotel," Mrs. Montgomery moaned. "I'd rather starve."

Wendy stifled a giggle, wondering whether she should reveal her presence and offer to fix the Montgomerys something to eat, or if she'd be better off staying out of sight till they left. Before she could make a decision, however, Mr. Montgomery spoke again.

"Mr. Underwood, please," he said. "He's expecting my call."

Wendy stood still, too curious about the connection between the contractor and Mr. Montgomery to move away, though she knew she should. Whatever involved the contractor might involve the stallion, too.

"Underwood? . . . Did you get it? . . . What do you mean, no? You promised me that I could see it this afternoon. . . . Good lord, man, you can't expect us to stay here indefinitely. . . . You weren't seen, were you?" There was a note of caution now in Mr. Montgomery's voice. "I can't take any risks, you know. I do have my reputation to protect. . . . Well, all right, but you'd better have it by tomorrow, or you can just forget the whole thing. The market for Indian relics is rather uncertain, and even what you described. . . ."

Wendy's gasp sounded like thunder in her own ears. Before she could move, the door was jerked open, and she was face to face with Mrs. Montgomery. Wendy jumped back, her leg throbbing in protest. Then she mastered her nerves.

"Mrs. Montgomery," she said, faking a yawn. "I thought I heard someone in the house, but I—I thought everyone was on the ride."

"I've never been on a horse in my life," Pamela Montgomery said, "and I certainly have no

124

intention of starting now. What are you doing here? Your aunt said there would be no one at home today."

Wendy gulped, aware that Mr. Montgomery was now standing behind his wife and his eyes were hard and angry. "I . . . I hurt my leg last night," Wendy said, "so I can't ride. I was just taking a nap and. . . ." She let it trail off, then made a great show of looking at her watch. "Could I fix you something to eat? Or. . . ."

"Oh, no—" Mrs. Montgomery began, but her husband interrupted ruthlessly.

"That's a wonderful idea," he said, a false smile not hiding the suspicion in his cold eyes. "We'd really appreciate that, wouldn't we, Pamela?"

Wendy felt an icy chill along her spine, but she could do nothing but smile back at him. "I'm not sure what Aunt Laura has in the refrigerator—" she began.

"I'm sure you'll manage," Mr. Montgomery said. "You seem to be a very bright young lady."

The words didn't soothe her, for Wendy sensed the threat behind them. Did he know that she'd

125

overheard him? Or had Mr. Underwood told him that she'd been on the island last night? Wendy swallowed hard, suddenly sure that what she'd felt on her back had been the hands of the contractor.

"If you'd just like to sit down in the living room," Wendy said, moving past them cautiously, "I'll see what I can find to eat."

"Why don't we keep you company in the kitchen?" Mr. Montgomery suggested, ignoring the shock in his wife's face. "With your—uh—bad leg, maybe we can be of help."

"You're very kind," Wendy murmured, frustration making her want to scream. She had to call Carol or Kirk or someone, but she didn't dare to with the Montgomerys sitting right there.

The next two hours were the longest she'd ever spent. Under the man's watchful eyes, she fixed a simple omelet with ham and onions and green peppers, just the way Aunt Laura had taught her. However, she could hardly swallow her own portion when Mr. Montgomery insisted that she eat with them. The warm English muffins tasted like sawdust, and her stomach

126

twisted as she wondered what the Montgomerys would do next.

She was ready to cry with relief when the sound of a car pulling up in front freed her from the tension for a moment. Only when she reached the front door did her joy fade. Sheriff Ramsey stood on the porch, and his face was grim.

"Where's your uncle, Wendy?" he asked when she opened the door.

Wendy took a deep breath, then glanced over her shoulder to see Mr. Montgomery standing in the archway between the living room and the dining room, well within hearing distance of her conversation.

"Everyone's off on a ride, Sheriff," she said, trying hard to sound normal. "Is there something I can do for you?"

The sheriff stared at her for a moment, then sighed. "What are you doing at home?" he asked suspiciously.

"I hurt my leg," Wendy explained.

"Hiking in the dark?" The words had a sarcastic edge, and Wendy held her breath, sure that she knew what was coming next and not wanting to hear it, especially not with the

127

already suspicious Mr. Montgomery standing so near.

"We—uh—had a beach party last night, and I fell into the lake," she lied.

"Well, in case you're planning some more beach parties, I think you should know that there was more damage done on Wild Horse Island last night. I've been told that there will be a guard on the island from now on, so I would advise you to find some other place for your—uh—parties."

"What about the Moonstone Stallion?" Wendy asked, unable to forget the horse she'd seen.

"My guess is the guard will shoot him, if he shows up," the sheriff said. "Besides, even a legend will have to give up after tomorrow."

"What do you mean?" Wendy asked, Mr. Montgomery forgotten.

"Tomorrow they start blasting out some of the rock for their foundations. That ought to get the Indian spirits out of the place." He paused and his eyes bored into hers. "And any other nosy little spirits that might be making visits. Do I make myself clear?"

Sick with fear, Wendy nodded.

"When Art gets home, tell him I'll be by tomorrow," the sheriff said, his eyes full of warning. "I still have to talk to him."

Wendy said nothing, but as she watched the sheriff walking away, she knew one thing. She couldn't just remain here. Somehow, she had to get out and get to Carol's house. Kirk and Little Elk had to be told. Something had to be done to save the Moonstone Stallion!

10 · A Desperate Plan

MR. MONTGOMERY was waiting when she turned around, and she knew from his gaze that he'd heard every word she and Sheriff Ramsey had said. Still, he smiled, without warmth, and asked, "Something I can do?"

Wendy forced an answering smile that was just as false as his had been. "I don't think so," she murmured. "If you'll excuse me now, I think I'll go lie down for a while. My leg. . . ."

"Don't worry about a thing," Mr. Montgomery said. "I'll be *right here* to answer the phone for you or attend to any other visitors. You just rest."

Wendy nodded, furious at the words *right here*. How in the world was she going to get out

130

of the house or even call anyone? As she limped down the hall to her room, she heard Mr. Montgomery telling his wife to relax on the front porch while he puttered around inside. The woman objected, but he whispered something that silenced her. In a moment, Wendy heard the front screen door close.

Wendy paced her room, glaring at her watch. The riders wouldn't be home till late afternoon, so there was no help coming from them. Carol wouldn't call till evening. It was already nearly three. A sound from the outside caught her attention, and Little Bit came leaping in through the open window.

Wendy looked at the nearby band of forest. The trees grew thick from here down to the barn, and from there. . . . A desperate plan began to form in her mind, and after only a few more minutes, she opened the window all the way and climbed over the sill. Her knee throbbed, but she ignored it, limping as quickly as possible toward the trees.

It took precious minutes to reach the far side of the barn and even longer to slip in through Happy Warrior's private paddock, which was at the opposite end of the barn from the house. Nimblefoot's bridle was hanging in the tack room, and she took it quickly. There was no time for a saddle, of course, but if she could slip into the corral from Happy's paddock and get Nimblefoot bridled. . . .

Wendy moved quickly, not sure what she thought the Montgomerys might do if she just rode off, but determined to go, no matter what. The first part was easy enough. She could see Mrs. Montgomery on the porch, but the woman didn't seem to notice the slight stir among the horses when Wendy joined them in the corral. Nimblefoot was easy to catch and bridle, even with Gypsy poking her delicate muzzle into Wendy's way every movement.

"I'll take you," she whispered to the filly. "Just keep quiet, all right?"

Leading Nimblefoot to the gate, Wendy unlatched it and let the filly out. Then she climbed up on the fence to mount, rode through, and turned the gelding back, to fasten the gate without dismounting. She heard Mrs. Montgomery's shout as she did so, but she wrapped her fingers in Nimblefoot's mane and

132

kicked him into a canter—on her way at last—
with Gypsy keeping up with every step!

She rode fast, using the lake route, not
because she hoped to see the Moonstone Stallion, but because she knew it was the fastest
way to reach Carol's house without being seen.
As she rode, she just prayed that her friend
would be home when Wendy arrived, instead of
off riding somewhere.

Carol was in the corral with Quito when she
rode up. "What are you doing here?" she asked,
her eyes running disapprovingly over the sweat-
wet gelding and filly. "I didn't think you'd be
riding for a couple of days."

"Go call Kirk and Little Elk and tell them to
come here as fast as they can," Wendy panted.
"We've got to do something. I'll explain, but
there's not too much time."

Carol's expression changed, and she ran to
the house without a word. Wendy slid off
Nimblefoot and nearly fell as her knee refused
to support her weight. She caught herself on the
corral fence, then handed Gypsy the tired
gelding's reins. "Walk him, Gypsy," she
ordered.

134

The filly looked startled, but the habits she'd learned while Wendy was training the Appaloosas were strong, and after a moment, she walked away, the gelding following her. Carol came back, looked at Wendy, then at the slowly pacing filly and gelding. "You'd better sit down," she said.

Wendy sank to the ground without argument. "What about Kirk and Little Elk? Are they coming?" she asked.

"They'll be over as soon as they can," Carol said. "Now, what's happened?"

Wendy took a deep breath and explained while they watched the filly walking the gelding to cool him off. By the time Wendy finished, Carol's dark eyes were snapping. "That horrible man!" she gasped. "What do you suppose he'll do, now that you've left the house?"

Wendy shrugged. "I wish I knew. Tell Mr. Underwood, I suppose."

"He can't do that for a while yet," Carol said quickly.

"What do you mean?" Wendy asked.

"Mr. Underwood's on the island with his crew. I saw them going out after lunch. They usually stay till around five or so. I always see the boat going back when I feed the stock."

"Then we can't do anything till they leave," Wendy said.

"What about the guard?" Carol asked.

"How many men went out?" Wendy asked instead of answering.

Carol considered. "The usual—four. I think there are only three men working with Mr. Underwood, so far."

"We'll just have to wait till they go back," Wendy said. "We can see then how many there are. Maybe he doesn't really mean to put a guard out there until dark—or maybe Mr. Underwood is planning to be the guard himself, at least until he gets whatever it was he was going to show to Mr. Montgomery."

"Do you think we should call the sheriff about it?" Carol asked. "Maybe he—"

"He'd never believe me," Wendy said. "He'd just say I was making trouble. He knows we were out there again, only he thinks we did a lot of damage. Mr. Underwood must have told him that."

Carol nodded. "You could be right. Kirk said

136

that the sheriff was out to talk to them, too. He said if it hadn't been for Dr. James, he thinks the sheriff might have really made some trouble, maybe even insisted that Little Elk go back home instead of staying here for the rest of the summer."

"If anything was wrecked, Mr. Underwood probably did it himself," Wendy snapped, her anger blazing again.

"Why would he do that?" Carol asked.

"So the sheriff would keep us off the island. He must have found something pretty super there, Carol, and maybe he thinks there's more." She smiled. "We sure ruined things for him last night."

"If he'd just let us get the stallion off safely," Carol murmured.

"But he doesn't believe in him," Wendy reminded her. "He hasn't seen him."

They sat in silence for a moment, then Carol asked, "What about your aunt and uncle? Did you leave a note or anything?"

Wendy sighed. "With Montgomery sitting in the dining room watching me?"

"So what are you going to do?"

137

"Nothing," Wendy said. "You'll have to do it. You call and ask for Gretchen. Mr. Montgomery volunteered to answer the phone, so you can ask him to have her call here as soon as she gets in. When she calls, I can have her tell Aunt Laura and Uncle Art. . . ." Her voice trailed off. "What shall I have her tell them?"

"How about telling them that I invited you over because my folks have driven down to Missoula on business and won't be back till some time tomorrow?"

"Is that the truth?" Wendy asked, realizing for the first time that she hadn't seen either of the Carters since she rode in.

"As a matter of fact, I was sort of hoping that you could spend the night with me—you and Gretchen. If you can't, I'm supposed to go in and stay with my Aunt Phyllis in town and. . . . Well, with everything going on here, I wasn't too crazy about going to town."

"Why didn't you say something before?" Wendy asked.

Carol sighed. "Up until last night, I wasn't sure I wanted Gretchen here. I mean, I'd heard about her fancy horse shows and her wonderful
138

half-Arab, till—"she giggled—"she made me feel as if I should take poor little Quito out and shoot him."

Wendy looked down at her hands. "You don't feel that way about Gretchen now, do you?" she asked.

"Not after last night. We really talked while you and the boys were cooking. She asked me about training and stuff, how it was to work with Quito." Carol's eyes were kind. "I think maybe she was just talking about the horse shows and stuff because she felt out of place here. Do you think that could be it?"

Wendy grinned. "She thought you didn't like her," she said softly.

"Well, I do," Carol said. "So I'll go call. Kirk and Little Elk should be here soon, so we can figure out what to do next."

"Right." Wendy leaned back against the fence, massaging her knee and watching the horses. Nimblefoot's black and white coat was dry, so she called Gypsy to her, getting up to check them both before she put them in the corral with Quito and the other Carter horses. That done, she limped to the Carters' front porch and sank down on one of the chairs, her knee aching.

Kirk and Little Elk came riding up in less than fifteen minutes. Carol brought out lemonade and cookies as Wendy told them everything that she'd heard and guessed. They listened in silence, but when she finished, Little Elk stood up. "I have to go out there," he stated. "Whatever he's found belongs to my people, not to that man Underwood."

"We can't go out there yet," Wendy counseled. "The whole crew is still on the island."

"When will they leave?" Kirk asked.

"They usually leave about five," Carol answered. "It's four-thirty now, so they should be leaving in about half an hour."

"I just hope—" Wendy began then stopped when the phone rang. Carol ran to answer it and summoned her at once.

"What's going on?" Gretchen demanded. "We rode in and there was nobody here. Your aunt is upset and. . . ."

"You're invited to spend the night at Carol's," Wendy said. "Let me talk to Aunt Laura and I'll set it up; then, please, get over
140

here as fast as you can. A lot has happened, and— Well, just hurry, okay?"

Gretchen sputtered a little, but in a moment Aunt Laura came to the phone. "Wendy, what is going on?" she asked, her tone telling Wendy that she was angry. "I thought your knee was too sore for riding, and then we came home and found Nimblefoot gone and—"

"I'm sorry," Wendy said. "I rode over bareback. It didn't hurt that way—I mean, not as much."

"Where are you?"

"Carol's," Wendy answered, glad to be on solid ground. "She called and said that her folks had to go to Missoula on business, and they won't be back till tomorrow, so she wondered if we could stay with her tonight. She was lonesome, so I rode over early, but if you need me. . . ." Wendy let it trail off, crossing her fingers.

"Why didn't Peg call me about it?" Aunt Laura asked.

Wendy bit her lip. "I don't know," she admitted. "Maybe it came up at the last minute or something. Anyway, you know Gretchen and

Carol haven't been exactly friendly, so I was hoping this—"

She heard her aunt's sigh and pictured her standing in the kitchen, still in her riding clothes. "Oh, all right, but you take it easy, promise? I don't want you doing any more damage to that knee."

"I'll be careful," Wendy assured her. "I'm sorry about not leaving a note. I fixed lunch for the Montgomerys, and then Carol called, and—"

"You fed the grand lady?"

Wendy could hear a giggle under the question and immediately felt better. More than anything, she wanted to share her fears with her aunt and uncle, but the weight of the sheriff's visit rested heavily on her shoulders. She knew that if she told them, she would be brought home at once, and the stallion. . . . She shivered at the thought of what might happen to the strange pale horse once the contractor began blasting on the island.

"I made them an omelet the way you showed me, and there were English muffins and coffee. For some reason, the Montgomerys didn't seem

142

too keen on Mrs. Gleeson's offerings."

This time the giggles became a laugh. "Then I suppose I should expect them for dinner tonight," Aunt Laura said.

"Probably," Wendy agreed, hoping fervently that her aunt was wrong. She didn't like to think about what Mr. Montgomery might say about her, or about the sheriff's visit. "Oh, will you pack my pajamas and stuff for Gretchen to bring over?" she added, forcing herself to be practical. "I rode over bareback, so I couldn't bring them with me."

"If we had a vacant bed, I'd ask Carol over here," Aunt Laura said. "See you tomorrow, and do be careful of that knee."

"Thanks so much," Wendy said. "And I do feel bad about leaving you short-handed to-night."

Aunt Laura laughed. "Don't worry; dinner won't be much. Most of our guests are so tired from the ride, I expect they'll fall asleep in their dessert."

Wendy hung up, wishing mightily that one of the people to fall asleep would be Mr. Montgomery. Still, she reminded herself, there

143

wasn't time to worry about that now. They had to get the stallion off the island before Mr. Underwood killed him. That was all that was really important.

11 · Relic

ONLY HER SORE LEG kept Wendy from pacing as they waited and watched the stretch of water where the boat from the island would have to pass. Little Elk was very restless, striding about, muttering angrily, then coming back to ask her again what she'd heard Mr. Montgomery say.

"He must have found a great treasure," Little Elk speculated. "What else could it be? What could have survived so long on that island without being discovered?"

Wendy shrugged, though she was aware that he wasn't really asking her. He left her, wandering down to the beach where the canoes waited, staring longingly toward the island.

Soon he came jogging back. "Gretchen's on

her way," he announced.

Wendy started to get up, but Carol pushed her back down on the chair. "I'll go meet her," she said. "You save your leg."

It pleased her to watch Carol and Gretchen as her two friends unsaddled Soot and brought the bulging saddlebags back to the porch. Gretchen flopped down on the porch beside Wendy's chair. "Now, will someone please tell me what is going on?" she asked. "Did you see the stallion again or something?"

Slowly, wearily, Wendy began the story once again. She had almost finished, when Carol suddenly jumped to her feet and ran to the end of the porch where she had placed her father's binoculars. In a moment they all heard the distant sound of a motorboat. Wendy held her breath, waiting till the blue and white boat appeared.

"One, two, three, four." Carol's voice rose as she counted. "We're clear!" she shouted. "As soon as they're out of sight, we can head for the island."

"So they didn't leave a guard," Wendy murmured, then shook her head. "That must mean
146

that Mr. Underwood is planning to come back himself. He's probably just going in to talk to Mr. Montgomery or to eat dinner."

"All the more reason to get out there now," Little Elk said. "Let's hope that whatever he found is still on the island."

"We've got to get the stallion off the island," Wendy reminded him. "Once the workers start blasting. . . ."

"If we can find him," Little Elk warned. "And if we can get near him once we do find him."

Wendy sighed, not even wanting to think about the other two trips, the way they had searched and searched and found no trace of the elusive creature. This time they had to find him, she told herself. The stallion's very life depended on it.

"All clear," Carol called from the beach.

"We'll have to post a lookout once we get to the island," Little Elk said. "If he's coming back, we sure don't want to let him catch us."

"I'll do it," Gretchen volunteered. "I wouldn't know what an Indian relic looks like, and as for that stallion. . . ."

147

"You're a good sport," Kirk told Gretchen as he helped Wendy into the canoe, then shoved it out into the lake. "I just hope we can come up with some idea of where that horse is hiding."

A wild whinny rang out and Wendy looked back in time to see Gypsy opening the corral gate. For a moment she considered going back, but there wasn't time. They could only hope that the horses would stay close to the corral and not disappear into the nearby forest. Gypsy came racing after them, plunging into the lake without any hesitation.

Wendy paddled hard, too worried even to apologize for the filly's behavior. It was her own fault, she realized. She should have remembered Gypsy's determination and her talent for opening gates, but she'd been too busy thinking about everything else.

Once they reached the island, Wendy was grateful for the filly's company, since she could use her back as a crutch on the walk from the shore to the pool. As they walked, she looked around, hoping for some sign of the stallion, but the woods, shadowy in the late afternoon, were silent. Her knee throbbed, but she was grimly
148

determined to ignore the pain.

"Okay," Little Elk said when they reached the area of the pool, "where did you hear the digging noise?"

Wendy limped forward till she was just where she'd been standing when she was knocked down the night before, then closed her eyes. "Over that way, I think." She pointed toward the brush that rose on the side of the pool opposite the waterfall. "It came from that direction, I'm sure."

"Let's look." Little Elk headed over toward the brush.

"I'm going to look for the stallion," Wendy said, still leaning on Gypsy.

"Where?" Carol asked, her eyes on the filly instead of Wendy. "If he was anywhere around, don't you think Gypsy would know?"

Wendy moved away from the filly and leaned against the nearest tree. "Too bad she isn't a dog, so I could tell her to find him," she observed with a sigh. "Where's your friend, Gypsy?" she asked. "Where's the stallion?"

Gypsy whickered and rubbed her nose along Wendy's arm, then began to graze calmly.

149

Wendy looked at Carol. "What do we do now?" she asked.

Carol shrugged. "You help Little Elk look for whatever Mr. Underwood found, and Kirk and I will see if we can find some sign of the stallion."

Wendy watched them go, very sure that they weren't going to find the horse. Feeling the pain in her bad leg even more than before, she limped along the edge of the pool and pushed her way through the brush to where Little Elk was searching the ground. "Find anything?" she asked.

"A man's footprints," Little Elk said. "Nothing else."

"But there was digging—" Wendy began, frowning. "I know I heard. . . ."

"I'll find it," Little Elk promised, his expression grim. "I won't let them steal that, too. They've already stolen our island."

Wendy watched him for several minutes, then turned away, still trying to remember last night. She limped back to where she'd been standing, and listened once again, hearing the splashing of the falls and the sounds of Little
150

Elk's movements in the bushes. Even the swish of Gypsy's tail was audible in the quiet afternoon. Then suddenly she remembered. She hadn't heard the digging sound when she reached the trees near the pool; she'd been off on the other side of the clearing.

Still concentrating, she hobbled across the sunny field, watching Gypsy as she grazed there. Once in the trees on the far side, she paused to listen. She could still hear the waterfall and the sounds Little Elk was making, and she knew at once that he was looking in the wrong place. The digging sounds had come from the right, closer to the pond and perhaps on the far side of it.

With that in mind, Wendy limped back across the meadow and made her way carefully along the rocky shore of the pond, past the scuffed-up place where she'd tumbled in, and then to the far side, where the ground was even more rocky. Here she saw the dry remains of a tree that had fallen, and beyond it, the freshly turned earth was like a scar against the needle-carpeted ground.

"Little Elk," she called. "Little Elk, over here."

151

Even as she rounded the fallen tree, she saw that the side of it was rotted and had been pulled away. The ground at the far end of the log had been disturbed, and there was a small trowel lying beside the turned earth. The moment he arrived, Little Elk dropped to his knees beside the fallen tree, caressing the torn bark carefully, almost tenderly.

"What is it?" Wendy asked.

"The Moonstone Chief must have hidden his treasure here," Little Elk said. "In the tree. That's why we never found anything."

"But Mr. Underwood did," Wendy reminded him.

Little Elk nodded and moved up to where the trowel lay. "And buried it here," he said. "He must have been digging it up last night when we got here, and when we all came racing through the woods, he just. . . ."

His voice died, and Wendy moved forward to look over his shoulder as he stopped digging with the trowel and began using his hands to scoop the soil away from a canvas-wrapped object. Very tenderly he lifted it out of the hole and shook the dirt from it; then he began to

unwrap it, his hands shaking.

For a moment Wendy just blinked, not recognizing what he held. Then she remembered the movies she had seen. "Is it a pipe?" she asked, staring at the long, slender object with its pale bowl.

"The Moonstone Chief's pipe," Little Elk said, his voice hushed with reverence. "I never dreamed. . . . Even Dad said it was long gone, but. . . ."

"He's coming! He's just leaving the dock!" Gretchen's voice rang out loudly in the stillness.

"We can't let Underwood have this," Little Elk exclaimed, leaping to his feet. "This belongs to my people. It is a tribal symbol, a priceless relic of our past. The Moonstone Chief was my great-great grandfather, and this was his. We can't let the pipe be sold to some dealer in Indian artifacts."

Wendy straightened painfully, suddenly conscious of her throbbing knee, then whistled for Gypsy. She knew that she'd make much better time if she again leaned on the filly during the walk to the shore, and there was obviously no time to waste. The filly came trotting around

154

the pool at once, then stopped, with her head turned, not toward them but toward the waterfall, her small ears pricked so sharply forward that their tips almost touched.

Kirk and Carol came out of the woods on the far side of the clearing just as Gypsy whinnied.

"Come on, Wendy," Little Elk urged. "If Underwood finds us here, he just might do something terrible."

"Let's go, Gypsy," Wendy said, touching the filly's shoulder.

Gypsy jumped nervously, then turned obediently as Wendy slipped an arm over her withers. Still, as they started around the pool, Gypsy looked back over her shoulder and whinnied once again.

Wendy put her other hand on the filly's nostrils. "You'd better be quiet," she warned. "If he hears you, he's liable to call the sheriff again. You'll get a reputation for being a real troublemaker."

It seemed to take forever as they hurried through the woods. The sound of the boat motor had died even before they reached the canoes, but there was nothing they could do

155

about that. Wendy led Gypsy into the water, praying that the filly wouldn't turn back now.

They paddled as fast as they could, trying not to look back, not to wait for shouts. Wendy was weak with relief when they finally pulled the canoes up on their beach and she could stumble across the sand with Gypsy's wet body beside her. She leaned against the filly until Carol, Kirk, and Gretchen herded the horses back into the corral. Once that was done, they all went into the house.

"What is it?" Gretchen asked. "What did you find?"

Little Elk said nothing, just placed the canvas-covered packet on the table and slowly unwrapped it. His fingers caressed the cold stone of the pipe, which was dark green at the top, and then changed halfway down to the pale, glowing moonstone that formed the remainder of the shaft and the large, carved bowl.

"It's our ancestral pipe," he said reverently. "The gift of the gods, passed on always to the leader of my people." He closed his eyes. "Last given to my great-great-grandfather, along with the colt whose coat was the same color as the

156

stone—the colt that later became known as the Moonstone Stallion."

As they peered at it, Wendy could see the battle scene that had been painstakingly carved in the stone bowl. Warriors battled, but one man stood out from the rest as he sat astride a powerful, rearing stallion.

"It's beautiful," she murmured, bending closer. "And that's our stallion. See, someone has carved his image into the stone."

"If only we'd found him, too," Kirk said. The others nodded their agreement, but no one offered any suggestions as to what they could do.

12 · Death Threat

THEY SAT IN SILENCE for several moments, then Kirk moved to the window. "You know," he said, "I don't think we'd better stay here."

"What do you mean?" Carol asked. "Gretchen and Wendy are staying here tonight."

"Where are your folks?" Kirk asked.

"Missoula. Daddy got a call this morning, and Mom decided to go with him. Why?"

"What if Mr. Underwood figures out what happened to the relic?" Little Elk inquired, his eyes meeting Kirk's.

"What'll we do?" Wendy asked, realizing at once what he meant.

"Couldn't all of you spend the night at your place, Wendy?" Kirk suggested.

158

"With good old Mr. Montgomery breathing down our necks?" Wendy asked.

"I'd forgotten him," Kirk said, returning to the table.

"I wish I could," Wendy murmured, her eyes still on the pipe, studying the horse that was so lovingly carved into the bowl of it. "We've got to get the stallion off the island," she said. "He's a part of this, too."

"How are we going to find him?" Carol asked. "Kirk and I looked everywhere, and—"

"He's got to be out there somewhere," Wendy interrupted.

"But where?" Carol moved to the window, then gasped.

"We've got to get out of here," she said.

"What do you mean?" Wendy asked, hurrying to join her.

"Look!" Carol pointed toward the lake, where a blue and white boat was heading toward their beach.

"What are we going to do?" Gretchen asked as they all ran toward the corral.

"Get into the badlands," Wendy said. "We can talk there."

159

Shouts from the lake followed them, but they were on their horses and racing away from the corral before the motor sound died. In a moment they were out of sight of the house. Kirk drew rein first. "What now?" he asked.

Wendy looked first at Little Elk. "Little Elk, can you prove that the pipe belonged to your ancestors?" she asked.

Little Elk studied the canvas-wrapped pipe he was still carrying, then nodded. "There's an old journal—my father showed it to me once. It belonged to a man who lived with my great-great-grandfather's tribe for a while. It mentions the pipe. He and my great-great-grandfather smoked it in friendship before the man died and everything got so bad for the tribe." He frowned. "Why?"

"Because I think you'd better go to Dr. James with that pipe—and maybe to the sheriff." Wendy looked back toward the lake. "It must be worth an awful lot of money, for Mr. Underwood to get Mr. Montgomery all the way out here from New York."

"It doesn't belong to Mr. Underwood," Kirk said. "He just found it on the island."

160

"And hid it again," Carol agreed.

Wendy nodded. "To keep the owner of the island from knowing about it, probably."

"Uncle Hal would know what we should do," Kirk said. "We'll let him tell the sheriff."

"What about you girls?" Little Elk asked. "What will you do?"

"I think maybe we could sleep in my room tonight," Wendy said. "We've got plenty of sleeping bags."

"But what about your aunt and uncle?" Carol asked.

"We'll just tell them we didn't want to stay here alone," Wendy said. "It's the truth, isn't it?"

Carol grinned. "I sure don't want to stay in my house tonight," she admitted.

"But what about the stallion?" Gretchen asked. "How are we going to get him off the island?"

Wendy looked around. "We can't go back tonight, not with Mr. Underwood looking for us, but maybe at dawn. . . . He doesn't have anything left to guard on his island now."

"And if we can't find the stallion?" Carol asked.

"We'll just stay on the island till we do,"

Wendy said. "They can't dynamite it if we're there, can they?"

Kirk grinned, but his eyes were sober. "Mad as he is now, I wouldn't count on it."

"Well, we'll figure something out in the morning," Wendy said. "Can you two meet us at the canoes before dawn?"

"We'll be there," Little Elk promised.

Kirk laughed. "There are advantages to being hired help. We get to live in the bunkhouse, so nobody pays too much attention to what time we get up. How about you?"

"We'll find a way," Wendy said, wondering even as she spoke what her aunt and uncle would say if she just told them the truth. "See you then."

"Be careful," Kirk called after them.

"Take good care of the pipe," Gretchen called in reply as they turned their horses toward the Cross R, pausing at the top of a small rise to wave to the two boys who were riding in the opposite direction.

They rode slowly toward the ranch house, Wendy favoring her leg, which throbbed its resentment at the treatment she'd been giving it. It was, she thought, hard to believe that it was still only a little past seven; so much had happened since she had ridden away only about four hours earlier.

When they reached the corrals, Cliff was just finishing feeding the horses. Wendy slid down carefully, then tried for a natural smile. "Where's Uncle Art?" she asked.

"He got called into town for a meeting," Cliff replied. "Your aunt call you to help her?"

Wendy shook her head. "Is something wrong?" she asked.

Cliff shrugged. "Dinner's pretty late, but maybe that's because of the long ride."

"Let me put the horses away," Carol volunteered. "You and Gretchen go on up to the house and help."

Wendy grinned at the brunet. "Thanks," she and Gretchen chorused as they hurried through the thick grass of the lawn and up the front porch steps.

The living room was full of guests. The television was blaring, and everyone looked rather impatient as Wendy and Gretchen said hello before hurrying through to the kitchen. Aunt

163

Laura turned from the stove at the sound of the swinging doors, and for a moment her usually happy expression looked decidedly stormy.

"What . . ." she began, but then just shook her head. "Don't tell me now. Just wash your hands and get the tables set. Wendy, could you make a green salad? The refrigerator went out sometime this afternoon, and the gelatin mold I left is completely ruined, along with several other things I'd planned for dinner."

Wendy nodded. "Is there anything else we can do?" she asked. "Carol will be here in a minute, so she can help, too."

"Thank goodness you came," Aunt Laura said, looking surprisingly close to tears. "When Art had to leave, I just didn't know what to do. I know the guests are starving out there, and—"

"How many, Mrs. Roush?" Gretchen asked from the dishwasher, where she was quickly unloading the dishes.

"Just the eight guests and the four of us, plus Cliff. George went to the cattlemen's meeting with Art. They said they'd get something to eat in town afterward."

"What happened to the Montgomerys?"

Wendy asked, realizing that they hadn't been sitting in the living room.

"I don't know what you fixed them for lunch, but it seems to have had a real effect," Aunt Laura said with a grin. "Mr. Montgomery called about half an hour after I talked to you and said they'd made other arrangements, that they were driving to Missoula late this evening so they could catch an early-morning flight out. He even left his check in the cabin—complete with an extra day's rent for all our trouble."

Wendy grinned. "I didn't think the omelet was that bad," she said, well aware that the food had nothing to do with the hasty departure. "But I guess they won't be missed."

"Oh, I don't know," Aunt Laura replied. "I think Mrs. Montgomery would be the only one who'd consider our late dinner proper. She was really shocked when I told her dinner was served promptly at six."

Carol came in and took over icing the cake that had been cooling on the counter, while Aunt Laura rushed between stove and cupboards, assembling the meal. In less than fifteen minutes they were ready to serve. For once

165

there were no comments about the strong scent of horses that followed the three girls as they moved from kitchen to dining room with the serving dishes, then took their own places at the plank family table.

When they were sitting down, Aunt Laura leaned back with a sigh. "Now, what brought you home? Besides my silent cries for help, I mean."

"We just decided that we didn't want to stay at Carol's alone," Wendy replied. "We decided we could sleep three across on my bed or maybe use one of the sleeping bags we have for our overnight rides."

"If you don't mind changing the beds and the towels, you can stay in style," Aunt Laura said. "Cabin Three is vacant now, you know."

"Terrific," Wendy said, thinking more of the dawn ride to Wild Horse Island than the night's comfort. "We can pretend we're guests."

"Not till after the dishes are in the dishwasher and that refrigerator is cleaned out," Aunt Laura warned. "I don't know what I'm going to do about keeping things cold for breakfast."

"Can't we store the milk and stuff in the

stream?" Wendy suggested. "That water is always cold."

"That's a wonderful idea," Aunt Laura said, looking relieved. "I don't know why I didn't think of that—except that I've been too busy to think about anything. When I opened that refrigerator and saw the gelatin mold. . . ." She shook her head, obviously not even wanting to think about it.

It was nearly nine before the kitchen and the refrigerator were completely cleaned up, but Wendy was grateful for the turmoil and confusion, for it kept her aunt from questioning her too closely about the events of the afternoon and early evening. Tomorrow, she promised herself. Once they had the stallion safely off the island, she'd tell her aunt and uncle everything.

Making up the cabin didn't take long, since the Montgomerys had used it very little the one night they had stayed in it. As they worked, Gretchen looked at Wendy. "Why do you think they left?" she asked, looking around the room.

Wendy shrugged. "Maybe they were afraid I'd tell someone about the phone call."

"But what about the pipe?" Carol asked.

167

"Probably he was planning to meet Mr. Underwood tonight. Maybe that's why Underwood came back to the island so soon. He sure didn't have time to eat before he showed up."

Gretchen nodded. "What do you think Mr. Montgomery will do now?" she asked.

"Get on a plane and get out of here," Wendy stated with confidence. "He was already telling Mr. Underwood how he had to protect his reputation and everything. I don't think he was very anxious to stay here."

"At least he isn't taking the pipe with him," Carol commented. "Did you see Little Elk's face when he was holding it? He must be awfully happy tonight."

"I'd be happier if we had the stallion, too," Wendy said. "Our getting the pipe off the island isn't going to keep them from blasting there tomorrow, and once they start. . . ."

"You don't think he'd just run away from the island, do you?" Gretchen asked. "I mean, he could swim to shore as easily as Gypsy, and if they start on the side near the docks—"

"I think he'll hide," Wendy said, frowning out the window of the cabin. "That's what he's

168

done every time we've gone out there, so why should he change now? You know how horses are; they do what they're used to. As far as we know, he's never left that island, however long he's been out there, so why would he do it now?"

Carol nodded. "And wherever he hides could be near where they'll be blasting," she finished.

Wendy sighed. "That's why we have to find him and get him away."

"So we'll go out at dawn and look till we find him," Gretchen said. "Maybe we can stage one of those sit-ins like they do on televison. Refuse to move till he's found."

"I hope it doesn't come to that," Wendy admitted, looking around. "Well, I guess that does it, and boy, am I glad! I'm beat, and dawn comes at a ridiculously early hour."

"Did you get the alarm clock?" Gretchen asked with a yawn.

"Oh, darn," Wendy said. "I forgot it."

"Want me to get it?" Gretchen and Carol both asked.

Wendy considered, then shook her head. "I'd better do it," she said, with a glance across at the darkened side of the big house. "It looks as if everyone has gone to bed, and I can go through without waking anyone up."

"Just don't wake us up when you come back," Carol teased, smothering a yawn.

Wendy slipped out into the cool night air and made her way across the rough grass to the silent house. She paused on the porch, then let herself in. She moved easily through the dark rooms, knowing them well after living there for nearly four months.

Only when she reached the door of her room did she pause, hearing her uncle's voice. "I'm glad the kids came back here to stay," he said. "I mean, besides being grateful they were here to help you."

"Why?" Her aunt sounded only mildly curious.

"I don't want them anywhere near that darned island tomorrow."

"Why not?"

"I was having dinner in the coffee shop when that contractor Underwood came in, and he was really steaming about something. The way he talked, I have a hunch there won't be much

170

island left after tomorrow. I just hope the corporation doesn't mind building on a heap of rubble."

"Why, that's terrible," Aunt Laura gasped, covering the moan that Wendy couldn't quite control. "I mean, surely. . . . Well, it's such a lovely place, and that must be why they wanted to build there."

"I don't know," her uncle went on. "I have a feeling that Mr. Underwood doesn't care about much of anything just now, and I don't have the slightest idea why."

Wendy smothered a sob, knowing only too well why Mr. Underwood was so angry, and sick at the thought that their finding and taking the pipe might have been the act that signed the death sentence for the Moonstone Stallion.

13 · The Stallion's Secret

WENDY STOOD in the dark hall for a moment more, but when nothing else was said about the island or Mr. Underwood, she slipped into her room, collected the alarm clock, patted both surprised-looking cats, and left again. As she crossed the dew-wet grass, she looked off to the west, where Wild Horse Island lay peacefully in the darkness. She longed desperately to return to the island, and search once more for the elusive stallion.

Once in the cabin, she told Carol and Gretchen what she'd overheard and watched the horror dawning in their faces. "He can't," Carol wailed. "We have to stop him."

"We have to get the stallion off the island,"

Wendy replied. "That's all we can do."

"So set the alarm," Gretchen ordered gently, "and come to bed. We're going to need all the strength we can get tomorrow."

Wendy nodded, but she was sure that she wouldn't sleep a wink. There was something, some clue that she had to remember, a clue that would help them find the stallion and bring him to safety.

In spite of her fears, she was asleep almost before her head touched the pillow. She neither thought nor dreamed from then till the shrilling of the alarm dragged her into worried wakefulness. She pulled herself out of bed at once, wincing as her stiff knee protested.

"I'm starving," Carol said, stretching and yawning.

"Lucky somebody does some planning," Gretchen teased. "While you two were getting the sheets and towels last night, I was bringing in supplies." She produced a half loaf of bread and jars of peanut butter and jelly. "If you'll go get some milk from the stream, we can have breakfast before we go."

"I'll get it," Carol said, before Wendy could

speak. "What about glasses?"

"There are some in the other room," Wendy replied. "All the cabins have them for the guests."

"Let's get moving then," Gretchen said.

They ate quickly, speaking little, though Wendy knew that the other two girls felt as she did about what lay ahead. "What's it like out this morning?" she asked Carol as she swallowed the second half of her sandwich.

"Misty again," Carol said. "I could hardly find the stream. I hope it clears up by the time we get to the island."

"Do you think we should take a halter or something for the stallion?" Gretchen asked.

"Just a rope, I think," Wendy said. "If he's as wild as he looked on the shore, we may have trouble even getting a rope on him."

"Kirk is a terrific roper," Carol reminded her. "Remember how well he did at the rodeo."

Wendy grinned. "That horse is a lot bigger than a calf, and Kirk won't have Apache to help him."

"We have to find the stallion first," Gretchen muttered, reminding the others of the biggest
174

problem that still lay ahead of them.

"So let's get started," Wendy suggested, washing the last of her food down with the remainder of her milk. "We want to be on the island by sunup, if we can."

"What about the boys?" Carol asked.

"They can join us, if they're late," Wendy answered. "We don't dare waste a minute."

They left the cabin, stepping into a world of smoky dimness as the mist wove itself through the trees and around the buildings, shifting slightly to reveal something, then just as suddenly closing over a tree or wall or. . . .

"What was that?" Carol gasped as the mist swirled around a dark, moving shape.

As if in answer a black head emerged from the mist.

"Soot," Gretchen gasped. "What in the world are you doing out here?"

Wendy felt her heart sinking. "Gypsy's done it again!" she wailed.

Carol whistled. In a moment Quito came trotting up to her, closely followed by Nimblefoot, but there was no third shape emerging from the mist, no answering whinny when

175

Wendy finally managed to whistle the familiar call. The filly had disappeared.

"What are we going to do about the rest of the horses?" Carol asked.

"Leave them," Wendy said, making a decision. "There's no way we can round up all of the horses in this mist. Somebody else will be waking up pretty soon; let them do it. The horses won't wander far—they haven't been fed their morning oats yet."

"What about Gypsy?" Gretchen asked. "Where do you suppose she is?"

Wendy closed her eyes, trying to deny what her instincts told her. "Probably on Wild Horse Island," she admitted bitterly. "I should have put her in the barn last night, but I didn't even think. . . ."

"I'll get the bridles," Carol offered, heading for the barn, the other two following more slowly, their horses at their sides.

"What about feeding them?" Wendy asked.

"We can leave them some oats at my place," Carol said.

The horses were quickly bridled, and Wendy mounted, using the corral fence once again. Her
176

leg throbbed, but she just bit her lip and ignored it. They rode off, scattering the ghostly horses as they headed for the gate to the lake pasture. Wendy wasn't at all surprised to find it open.

"Just follow the open gates and find the missing horse," she muttered bitterly as she turned Nimblefoot back and secured it once again. "Uncle Art is going to be furious."

"By the time he finds out what we've been up to, he won't have time even to think about Gypsy," Gretchen said sadly. "He'll probably put me on the next plane back to Arizona."

Wendy sighed. "I'm sorry about this, Gretchen," she apologized. "It sure isn't the vacation I planned when you said you were coming, but—"

"Hey, I wasn't complaining," Gretchen assured her. "I've had a fantastic time, and if I can help save that horse. . . . When I tell everybody back in Phoenix about this, they'll be positively green."

"I'm glad you're here to help," Carol said, and Wendy smiled in spite of her worries. "I just hope we can do something."

They rode in silence for a while, and Wendy

found her mind returning to yesterday's fast escape from the island. There'd been something. . . . They reached the beach before she'd been able to pinpoint whatever it was.

While Carol checked the house, which they'd left open in their hurried flight from Mr. Underwood, Wendy and Gretchen turned the three horses loose in the corral and fed all the stock. By that time the sky was growing a little lighter, and they knew it would soon be dawn. They walked slowly to the beach, carrying a bucket of oats and a heavy rope.

"I sure hate to go without the boys," Carol said.

Wendy and Gretchen nodded their fervent agreement.

"I wonder what time the construction crew will be out," Gretchen murmured.

Carol answered, "They usually cross over between seven-thirty and eight."

Wendy looked at her watch. "That gives us about two hours," she said.

Carol sighed. "We'd better go."

It was an eerie trip, for the mist still lay on the lake, and after a certain point, they could see

179

neither the shore nor the island. Still, the rising sun gave them a direction, and they paddled steadily, finally breaking through a band of mist to see the green shore. A plaintive whinny greeted them, and Gypsy came cantering along the narrow strip of sand, looking nearly as wild as the island.

"Well, at least she's here," Carol said. "Now, where. . . ."

The stallion's neigh drew their eyes to the trees, and for a moment they could see a flash of his pale hide before he disappeared into the misty forest. They renewed their paddling, grounding the canoe roughly and stumbling ashore. Gypsy came trotting up to greet them.

Wendy gave the filly a couple of handfuls of oats before pushing her away. "Those are for your shy friend," she told the filly. "Now, please show us where he is."

Gypsy tried to reach the bucket once more, then moved away without argument, disappearing into the trees. The three girls plunged after her, Wendy limping painfully but unwilling to slow the filly to use her as a crutch. She wanted Gypsy to go after the stallion—to lead

180

the three girls to his hiding place.

They moved through the mist-draped trees, slowing when the filly paused to grab a mouthful of grass, then speeding up when Gypsy did. A light breeze was rising, and even as they crossed a small meadow, the mist was lifting and tearing, spreading upward so they could see in all directions again. Not that there was anything to see. The stallion had once again done his disappearing act.

No one was really surprised when they emerged in the meadow near the pool. Gypsy, as she had so frequently before, began to graze on the already short grass, showing no interest in wandering off. The three girls looked around, frustrated.

"Now what?" Gretchen asked.

Carol sighed. "You and I go looking, I guess," she said. "Wendy can stay here and keep an eye on Gypsy, just in case we scare up that ghost horse."

"I can look, too," Wendy protested. "I'm not going to just sit here and wait!"

"Hey, how's it going?" Kirk and Little Elk came striking into the clearing, grinning. Their grins faded as they looked at the girls' faces.

It took only a moment to tell the boys what Wendy had overheard from her uncle. They were grim-faced when she finished. "You stay here, Wendy," Kirk said, echoing Carol's words. "We need someone here to watch Gypsy. She's still the only one that might be able to lead us to the stallion."

"But—" Wendy started to protest.

Little Elk raised a hand, stopping her. "We'll each take a quarter of the island and search our way back here. If he tries to go by, Gypsy will hear him or see him, and you can follow him. All right?"

Wendy wanted to argue, but after a moment, she recognized the logic of the boys' plan. "I guess I *am* too slow to be much help," she admitted. "I'll keep my eyes open."

"Let's just hope there's something to see," Carol said grimly. In a moment Wendy was alone in the clearing, except for the calmly grazing filly.

Wendy watched Gypsy for several minutes, then turned away and carried the oat bucket around the end of the pool, to where the fallen tree made a comfortable seat for her. From there she could not only watch Gypsy but also see the whole surrounding area, from the falls to the farthest edge of the meadow.

Nothing stirred but the trees as the morning breeze removed the last of the mist and the sun began to burn off the dew. Gypsy switched a fly away with her long tail, then ambled to the pool for a drink.

Suddenly there was a faint sound from beyond Gypsy, and the filly turned, staring at the falls. Wendy followed her gaze, and at once the memory that had been eluding her snapped back into her mind. Gypsy had been looking at the falls just before they left the island last time, and she'd been whinnying to someone or something.

Wendy got to her feet and limped to the edge of the pool, staring more closely at the falls. The rocks on each side were wet and dark, but the area behind the water was darker, formless. Wendy moved closer, and as she did so, she saw something that she hadn't noticed before. There was a wide ledge leading from the rocky shore of the pond to the falls.

Wendy considered it for a moment, then went back and picked up the oat bucket. Taking a deep breath, she began moving along the ledge, noticing that the rock was well worn. The water splashed down on her, cold in the cool morning air, but she didn't stop till she reached the full rush of it. Then she tried to see through the silvery curtain of water.

Something stirred in the shadows, and, taking a deep breath, Wendy plunged through the veil of water and into the darkness beyond. The pale horse leaped away from her, crowding against the damp rear wall of the small cave, his head toward her, ears flattened against his skull.

Realizing the danger of her position, Wendy stood perfectly still. "Easy, big boy," she murmured, trying to keep her voice from shaking. "It's all right. I'm not here to hurt you. I just brought you something to eat." She shook the oats in the bucket.

The horse stood his ground. Wendy shook the oats again. One pale ear came forward. Slowly, carefully, Wendy dipped a hand into the oats and then extended it toward the horse. The space behind the falls was so small, she could

184

almost reach out and touch him.

It seemed forever that they were suspended in the water-noisy tension of the cave, then she felt the soft whisper of his breath, and the oats were being licked off her palm. Slowly, not wanting to startle him, she dipped her hand in and offered him some more.

As her eyes adjusted to the darkness, she became aware of a number of things. The horse was big, but very thin; his pale coat was rough and uncared-for; and the long forelock hung over his eyes when he lowered his head a little.

"Poor boy," Wendy said, setting the oat bucket down. "You've missed a lot of meals, haven't you?" Very carefully, she touched his neck.

The horse shuddered away from her touch, but she kept her fingers lightly against the warm hide till the horse accepted them; then she stroked him lightly as he ate. "You're going to have a lot more meals, boy," she said. "We're going to take you off this island now, and then you'll be safe."

The horse lifted his head and Wendy picked up the bucket, well aware that she had to get

186

him out of the cave before he finished the oats. "Come on, boy," she said, moving toward the waterfall barrier. "Let's go out in the sun so I can put a rope on you before the food's all gone."

To her surprise, the horse followed her willingly enough all the way to the fallen tree where she'd left the rope. Once there, however, she wasn't so sure what to do—how to get the rope on the big animal without frightening him, and what to do once she had it on his strong neck.

Up close and out in the light, she could see a great deal more about the mysterious stallion. He was a handsome animal, in spite of his poor condition. If he was well fed and cared for, she had a feeling he would show the marks of good breeding. She patted him again and was glad to see that he didn't shy away from her touch.

"You're not really wild, are you?" she asked gently. "Or at least you weren't always."

Wendy bent to pick up the rope, but as she did so a shout broke the peaceful scene. "Run, Wendy," Carol shouted. "Take Gypsy and run."

Wendy spun around, conscious of the huge

187

stallion beside her. He turned, too, the oats forgotten as his dark eyes widened to show a ring of white. Wendy gasped as Mr. Underwood suddenly broke free of the trees, a rifle in his hands. She screamed as he pointed it at the peacefully grazing filly.

14 · Killer Stallion

No!" WENDY SCREAMED. She tried to run around the pool, but her knee gave way, and she fell heavily. As she did so, she saw Kirk grabbing at the rifle as the big man shook him off. Then something leaped over her, and she heard the stallion's squeal of rage. It was followed almost at once by a man's yelp of terror. The rifle exploded like thunder in the morning's quiet air.

Frightened, Wendy scrambled to her feet. Her eyes went first to Gypsy, who was now standing on the far side of the clearing, obviously poised for flight, but unharmed. Then she heard a shout and turned to see the sheriff and her uncle striding into the clearing.

"What is going on here?" demanded Uncle

Art as Kirk handed Underwood's rifle to the sheriff.

For the first time Wendy noticed that Mr. Underwood was now lying on the ground. Even as she watched, the man struggled to his feet. "Give me my gun," he snarled. "That animal tried to kill me."

"What animal?" Uncle Art asked. "Gypsy?"

Wendy looked around and realized that the stallion had disappeared once again. "You didn't shoot him?" she gasped, limping quickly around the pool to join the others as they came out of the trees.

Little Elk grinned at her. "That was the only casualty," he said, pointing to a torn place near the top of a nearby pine. "The stallion hit him before he could fire."

"You saw him?" Wendy asked.

Little Elk nodded. "He went by me like a freight train. Where did he come from? How did you find him?"

"Hold it," Sheriff Ramsey said. "Just what is going on here? What are you kids doing here? And you, Underwood, what are you doing chasing around this island with a rifle?"

190

"These brats are trespassing," Underwood said, his gray eyes narrowing as he looked around. "And not for the first time. They're the ones who've done all the damage here. I want you to order them off. I have three men and a lot of dynamite coming out here in about an hour, and I want these troublemakers off this island."

"As soon as we catch the Moonstone Stallion, we'll leave," Wendy agreed.

"Now listen here, Wendy," the sheriff began, "there's no such horse—"

"Oh, yes there is," Carol broke in. "Ask Mr. Underwood. The stallion ran him down because he was trying to shoot Gypsy."

"Is that true?" the sheriff asked, turning to Underwood.

The blond man moved restlessly. "There was a horse," he admitted grudgingly. "A big, crazy one. He charged at me. He tried to kill me. He should be shot."

"Is that true, Wendy?" Uncle Art asked. "Did you really find the stallion here?"

Wendy nodded. "I found his hiding place," she said quietly, "but he's not a killer. I was just

191

about to put a rope on him when—" she shivered at the memory—"when Mr. Underwood came and tried to shoot Gypsy."

"Where is the horse now?" Sheriff Ramsey asked.

Kirk shrugged. "He ran into the trees."

"Where did you find him?" Carol asked.

Wendy grinned. "Gypsy told me where to look," she said. "I just didn't listen before, but today, while I was sitting on that fallen tree. . . ." She let it trail off and met Mr. Underwood's cold glare.

For a moment he just stood there, then he turned to the sheriff. "If you'll give me my rifle, I'll go back for my crew."

"What about them?" The sheriff waved a hand at Wendy and the rest of the group.

"Get them off this island before I get back or I swear I'll have 'em all arrested. And I'll shoot that blasted horse, too." Mr. Underwood grabbed his rifle and, without a backward glance, stalked off into the trees.

"Wendy," Uncle Art began, "what are you doing out here?"

Wendy looked up at him, feeling guilty. "Let

192

me find the stallion first," she said. "It won't take Mr. Underwood long to get his men. . . . Oh, Uncle Art, he's such a beautiful horse, and he's not a killer really. I mean, I was in the cave with him and—"

"Cave?" Gretchen broke in.

"Behind the falls," Wendy said. "That's where he was hiding. That's why Gypsy hung around here all the time. She knew where he was."

"Well, what do you want to do?" her uncle asked, with a sigh of surrender.

"Find him again and get a rope on him," Wendy said. "Then we'll have to figure out a way to get him off this island and safely away from Mr. Underwood."

"Once you get him off this island, there are a lot of questions you're going to have to answer," Uncle Art warned her.

Wendy nodded. "I know," she said, "and I want to, but right now—" She paused, then asked, "How did you get here?"

"When I woke up to a yard full of horses but no Gypsy and Nimblefoot, what else would I think?" he asked. "I called the sheriff, and he

193

picked me up on the shore in his boat. We must have landed just behind Underwood. We heard the shouting and that shot."

Wendy closed her eyes, remembering the moment and the terror that had nearly destroyed everything. Then she forced the memories away and opened her eyes. "We've got to find the stallion," she said. "We've got to get him away before Mr. Underwood comes back."

"How?" Sheriff Ramsey asked.

Wendy nibbled at her lip. "He's always come to his hideaway," she said, trying to think. "Maybe if you all spread out around the island and look for him, he'll come back and I can catch him."

"Wouldn't it be better if I roped him?" Uncle Art asked. "We brought a rope, and if he's a big horse and wild. . . ."

"Let me try first," Wendy said, her eyes meeting his. "He let me touch him before, and I'll have the oats and Gypsy."

"You just be careful," her uncle cautioned. "I don't like to see horses shot, but I'd rather have the beast destroyed than to have one of you children hurt. Is that clear?"

194

Wendy nodded, whistled for Gypsy, and leaning on the horse's sturdy back, returned to the fallen log where the rope and the bucket of oats waited. She was still shaking inside from the shock of what had almost happened to the filly, and once everyone left the clearing, she leaned against the warm reddish brown shoulder and let her tears wash into Gypsy's rough mane.

The filly nuzzled her shoulder, blowing her warm breath into Wendy's dark blond hair till her sobs changed to giggles. "Okay, silly filly," she said. "I guess you do get enough baths swimming out here to visit your ghostly friend. But no more, understand? We're going to take him off the island, and you've got to stay away from here from now on."

The eyes, one dark, the other blue, regarded her solemnly, then suddenly the filly lifted her head and turned to look over her shoulder. Wendy followed her gaze just in time to see the stallion step cautiously out of the trees.

"Hi, fella," she called. "Ready for some more oats?"

The stallion took a step in her direction, then stopped and turned, his ears snapping back against his head. Wendy caught her breath as the sheriff stepped out, swinging a rope. He tried to throw it, but the stallion was already plunging at him, bellowing in rage. The sheriff stumbled awkwardly out of the horse's path, then fell heavily into a thornbush as the stallion disappeared in the brush again. Shaken, Wendy ran over to him as quickly as her bad leg would allow.

"That's the horse you're going to rescue?" the sheriff asked, his face red with anger. "I'm beginning to think Underwood might have the right idea."

"No, he's not like that with me," Wendy explained. "Please, you said I could have a chance. Just stay away from him, please!"

The sheriff got up and brushed himself off, some of the anger draining from his face. "Don't worry, I'm not going to play cowboy with him again," he said rather stiffly. "But I'm going to stay right here in the trees, and if he shows any sign of attacking you, you just stay out of my line of fire—hear?"

Sick at heart, Wendy could only nod; there wasn't time to argue. She returned once more to

196

her place on the log, waiting and hoping that the stallion would return again and give her one last chance to save him from certain death.

This time she hadn't long to wait. She heard the soft sounds in the brush even before Gypsy turned. She picked up the oat bucket, leaving the rope where it was. The stallion approached warily, his dark eyes surveying the area before he left the cover of the trees. His moonstone coat was damp in spots, and his eyes still held a trace of wildness, but when Gypsy whickered a greeting, he began a cautious approach.

Wendy talked to him, not really conscious of what she was saying, aware that the words weren't important, that only the sound of her voice and the love she felt for the proud, wild creature meant anything. When he was close enough, she set the bucket down beside the rope, then touched his damp neck. He shivered, but he stayed.

"I'm going to have to put a rope on you," she told him softly. "It won't hurt you, but you have to leave the island, and that's the only way we can do it. Please understand." She bent and picked up one end of the rope, lifting it slowly

198

till it touched his neck. He shuddered, but her voice and the oats held him as she eased it around and knotted it high on his neck, waiting till he lifted his head to loop the rope around his muzzle and tie it again into a rough halter.

"Now what?" Sheriff Ramsey asked.

The stallion jumped, but he didn't fight the rope when Wendy held him.

"Are you still here?" Mr. Underwood's voice jarred them all. Wendy had to bite her lip to keep from screaming her frustration.

"Stay back," she warned, keeping her voice as low as she could. "If he sees you. . . ."

Sheriff Ramsey moved out of the trees, well away from where Wendy stood with the two horses. "That horse was found on Wild Horse Island, Underwood," he said. "Do you want to claim him for the company that bought the island?"

Wendy held her breath, her fingers tightening on the rope till they ached with the strain. Mr. Underwood moved out into the clearing, too, and for a moment his eyes met hers. She could almost feel the hatred in them.

"He's not worth a bullet," he answered at

199

last. "The brats are welcome to him. I hope he teaches them some respect. But you have to get him off *now*—or, so help me, he's one dead horse. You got that?"

"Everybody just stay back," Wendy warned. "Give us plenty of room, and I'll take him to the shore."

"Let us go ahead of you and get the canoes out," Little Elk suggested, speaking from surprisingly close at hand. "You can lead him into the water and across the lake."

Wendy looked at the stallion, aware that he had turned toward Little Elk, but he showed no reaction, none of the viciousness that he'd shown toward the sheriff and Mr. Underwood. Wendy nodded. "Go ahead," she said. "I can't walk very fast, anyway."

It was a long walk to the shore, and Wendy was grateful for every step of it, for she realized that the greatest test still remained. It was one thing to lead the pale stallion through his quiet island, but when they reached the shore. . . . He had refused to leave his island for a long time, so how could they force him to do it now? Yet if he didn't, Mr. Underwood still waited with a rifle.

15 · Escape!

THE STALLION STOPPED at the edge of the beach. Wendy tried enticing him with the few remaining oats, but he only looked beyond her to the canoes. Wendy pulled on the rope halter, and the ears flipped back against the horse's skull.

"Do you want us to try driving him in?" Little Elk asked from the canoe he shared with Carol and Gretchen. "Maybe if we got behind him and made a lot of noise. . . ."

"I think he'd attack," Wendy said, remembering how he'd run at both the sheriff and Mr. Underwood. "He's a fighter."

"So what do we do?" Carol asked.

Wendy looked at the pale hair on the bony back. There were white patches, rubbed spots that had grown back in a different color. They showed now in the sunlight of late morning—they were saddle marks!

She heard the distant sound of a boat motor and guessed that it would be her uncle and the sheriff coming around the island to see what had happened. If they decided to help her, she was sure that the result would be a tragedy.

Without giving herself time to think, she handed the rope to Gypsy. "Lead him, Gypsy," she said. Then she scrambled onto the startled stallion's back, using a nearby log to mount.

She felt the lean muscles tense and sat very still, winding her fingers gently in the long, heavy mane. "It's all right, boy," she said. "It's just me up here, and I'm not going to hurt you. Just don't buck now. Just relax and let me ride you. You've been ridden before, so I know you understand." She lifted her head. "Call Gypsy, Carol," she instructed, not raising her voice any more than she had to.

The faces turned her way were pale and blank with shock, but after a second, Carol found her voice and called the filly. Kirk and Gretchen added their voices and began to paddle away from the island.

"Go, Gypsy," Wendy ordered, feeling the hump in the stallion's back as it eased a little, accepting her light weight. "Go home!"

Slowly, dubiously, the filly moved forward till the rope tightened between her and the stallion. Very cautiously, Wendy touched her heels to the stallion's sides and leaned forward. "Let's go, big boy," she said. "It's time for you to go home, too."

For a moment it all hung in the balance, then Gypsy snorted and pulled the rope, plainly puzzled because the stallion didn't follow her as Nimblefoot and the young Appaloosas always did. The stallion shuddered, then took the first step, crossing the sand and finally following the filly into the lake.

Wendy stayed with him till he began to swim strongly, following Gypsy, then she let herself slide off; she began to swim, too, heading for the motorboat where her uncle and the sheriff still waited. She could see anger and relief mixed on her uncle's face as he pulled her into the boat.

"Please take me to Carol's," she said. "I'll come home as soon as the stallion is safe, but

I've got to be waiting there for him when Gypsy brings him ashore."

"That was the craziest thing you've ever done," her uncle exploded. "He could have killed you. How did you know he wouldn't buck?"

"He had saddle marks," Wendy explained. "Old white patches from where a saddle had rubbed his withers. And he has scars, Uncle Art, lots of them, so maybe he's been hurt or abused. Maybe that's why he doesn't like men with ropes and guns. But he trusts me."

"He's no scruffy Indian pony," Uncle Art conceded, and Wendy could hear the change in his voice, the dawning interest. "What about a brand?"

Wendy thought for a moment, then shook her head, her eyes never leaving the two horses' heads that rose above the blue of the lake. "I didn't see one," she said. "We'll know more when we get him into a stall and cleaned up and fed."

"You can't bring him home, Wendy," Uncle Art reminded her, his voice gentle.

"I know that," Wendy replied. "The Cross R belongs to Happy Warrior. He'd never allow
204

another stallion on the place."

"Carol's parents might not be too thrilled to have a stallion in their barn, either," Uncle Art warned her. "He's not like Happy."

Wendy looked across the water to the blue canoe and Little Elk. "I have a feeling that everything we found on the island should go to Little Elk," she murmured. "His great-great-grandfather brought the first Moonstone Stallion to the island, so why shouldn't Little Elk have this one?"

"Everything?" The sheriff's voice had an edge to it. "What else did you find out there?"

Wendy swallowed hard, then described the pipe and its connection to Mr. Montgomery and Mr. Underwood.

The sheriff's face darkened as she spoke, and when she finished, he exploded. "There's going to be no blasting on that island today," he said. "I'm going right back and stop all activity till there's a full-scale investigation. Finding that pipe proves it was a burial place, so we should be able to work out something with the new owner of the island."

"You won't take the pipe or the stallion away

from Little Elk?" Wendy asked, frightened by what she'd done.

"That will be settled in the courts," the sheriff replied. "At least the pipe will. The horse probably won't be claimed."

"They both should belong to Little Elk's people," Wendy protested.

"We'll talk about it later," Uncle Art said as they reached the shallow water and Wendy climbed over the side of the boat. "You come home as soon as you get things settled, hear?"

Wendy nodded. "I'll call if it's going to be very long," she assured him. "And thanks, Uncle Art . . . for understanding."

Their eyes met for a moment, and Wendy felt the warmth of his love. She was grateful that his anger at her wasn't deep enough to make him endanger the horse. She deserved punishment, she knew, but Uncle Art would wait till the stallion was safe.

It took several hours, but in that time, they learned a great deal. The stallion was shy, but he soon accepted the friendship offered by Carol, Gretchen, Kirk, and Little Elk. Only when Dr. James arrived, having been called by

Kirk, did his aggressiveness return, and it took all their patience to force him to accept the touch of a grown man's hand.

The veterinarian made a slow, careful examination of the big horse; then Little Elk and Wendy put him in a stall with plenty of hay, oats, and fresh water before following the others to the kitchen of the Carter house. Carol poured lemonade and put out the plate of brownies that her mother had left them the day before.

"What do you think, Dr. James?" Little Elk asked.

"He's in poor condition, but I think that's mostly from being on the island. Good food and love should take care of a lot of it. He's not a young horse. I'd guess about fifteen or sixteen, but I won't know for sure till I can get a better look at his teeth."

"Do you think he can ever be gentled?" Little Elk asked.

"He'll never be a pet," Dr. James said. "He's been too ill-used ever to be a safe horse to keep around a lot of people."

"What about on a ranch?" Wendy asked.

207

Little Elk's eyes met hers. "My father has some fine mares and plenty of pasture land. If I returned to him with the pipe and the stallion. . . ." He paused and grinned sheepishly. "I know he's not the real Moonstone Stallion, but he is the right color, and he's wild and free."

Dr. James shrugged. "Let's take him to our barn and give him a chance," he said. "If he can learn to trust me, maybe there's hope for him."

Wendy slumped back in the chair, relaxing at last. She knew the vet well enough to know that the stallion would be safe; he was a man who cared deeply about his four-legged patients.

"Where do you think he came from?" Carol asked, reaching for a brownie. "I don't recall any horse like him around here, do you, Doc?"

Dr. James sipped his lemonade. "I don't know," he said. "I seem to remember something about a wild stallion. I think it was six, seven years ago. There was a rodeo passing through the area. Anyway, one of those big stock carriers hit a patch of ice on the road or something and got kind of smashed up. I went out to tend to the animals, and there was a lot of
208

talk about one of the bucking horses having gotten away—one they called the Ghost Stallion."

Wendy thought of the stallion's violence, his apparent hatred of men, and nodded. "Maybe that's why he trusted me so easily," she commented.

"If he is that horse, you could be right," Dr. James agreed. "I don't even remember what the animal was supposed to look like, just that it was a stallion and supposed to be pretty vicious and hard to handle."

They sat in silence for a moment, then Dr. James leaned forward, taking another brownie and turning his attention to Little Elk. "What about the pipe?" he asked. "Did you say anything to the sheriff about it?"

Wendy squirmed a little. "I'm afraid I did," she confessed. "Once he heard, he said he'd go back to the island and stop them from blasting. He said that the owner would have to be contacted, because finding the pipe proves the island was an Indian burial ground."

Dr. James nodded. "It had to be told," he assured her. "I think Little Elk has a good claim if his father does have documents mentioning the pipe. It's valuable because of its history, and his people were a part of that history."

Little Elk nodded. "The whole tribe will be united in the claim," he said. "It's a tribal treasure."

"That will all come out in the courts," Dr. James said, "but now I've got to get back home." He stood up. "Boys, do you think you can get the stallion to the ranch without getting into trouble?"

Little Elk nodded. "I won't let anything happen to him," he promised. "He's going home, where he belongs."

"He'll finally be free," Wendy said. "No more hiding or starving in the winter."

"Not for the Moonstone Stallion," Little Elk agreed. "Once I get him home, he'll be the pride of the tribe. If it hadn't been for him, our ancestral pipe would have been lost forever."

Wendy got up, too, wincing. "I guess we'd better be getting back, Gretchen," she said.

"I hope your uncle won't be too angry at you," Carol murmured.

"I think he understands," Wendy said. "He was just very worried about me, about all of us, but now everything is all right."

"It really is, isn't it?" Carol shook her head in wonder. "We did it—we saved the Moonstone Stallion!"

"I'm going to say good-bye to him for now," Wendy said, "but we'll be over to see him as soon as we can, Little Elk."

"Anytime," Little Elk agreed. "He was your horse first, you know."

"Gypsy is all the horse I need," Wendy replied, giggling. "I must have been out of my mind to get on that big horse. If Gypsy hadn't been there to lead him. . . ."

"I think you are all a little crazy," Dr. James said, smiling at them. "Horse-crazy."

They laughed as they walked out into the sunshine where Gypsy was waiting, her bright, mismatched eyes looking from one face to another as though she, too, wanted to share the joke. Unable to, she whirled and raced, bucking, around the yard, her sorrel coat glowing. Then she came dancing back to offer herself to Wendy as a crutch as Wendy limped to the corral. It was time to go home.

YOU WILL ENJOY

THE TRIXIE BELDEN SERIES

31 Exciting Titles

TRIXIE BELDEN MYSTERY-QUIZ BOOKS

2 Fun-Filled Volumes

THE MEG MYSTERIES

6 Baffling Adventures

ALSO AVAILABLE

Algonquin
Alice in Wonderland
A Batch of the Best
More of the Best
Still More of the Best
Black Beauty
The Call of the Wild
Dr. Jekyll and Mr. Hyde
Frankenstein
Golden Prize
Gypsy from Nowhere
Gypsy and Nimblefoot
Gypsy and the Moonstone Stallion
Lassie—Lost in the Snow
Lassie—The Mystery of Bristlecone Pine
Lassie—The Secret of the Smelters' Cave
Lassie—Trouble at Panter's Lake
Match Point
Seven Great Detective Stories
Sherlock Holmes
Shudders
Tales of Time and Space
Tee-Bo and the Persnickety Prowler
Tee-Bo in the Great Hort Hunt
That's Our Cleo
The War of the Worlds
The Wonderful Wizard of Oz